Mary Costello Caldbeck

Sefton Hall

A tale. Vol. 1

Mary Costello Caldbeck

Sefton Hall
A tale. Vol. 1

ISBN/EAN: 9783337088859

Printed in Europe, USA, Canada, Australia, Japan

Cover: Foto ©Andreas Hilbeck / pixelio.de

More available books at **www.hansebooks.com**

A TALE.

IN TWO VOLUMES.

BY THE LATE

MARY COSTELLO CALDBECK.

VOL. I.

London:

T. CAUTLEY NEWBY, PUBLISHER,
30, WELBECK STREET, CAVENDISH SQUARE.
1870.

SEFTON HALL.

CHAPTER I.

"I AM glad to meet you, Harry. Will you come to Sefton to-morrow?"

"Is it to the meet? Why, I am off to town to-morrow, my dear fellow."

Harry was always going to town; indeed, though he talked a good deal of sport, his cousin suspected him of any day preferring the theatres, clubs, and so forth, to a pleasant day's ride, or a good day's shooting. Harry had some excuses for finding town, as he

called it, pleasant ; he owned a good property, which had been carefully nursed for
him through a long minority, which property,
by the way, was just beginning to feel those
constantly recurring visits to town. He was
good-looking, and had that happy, merry disposition which greatly contributes to make
people welcome in society, and which certainly enabled him to enjoy the welcome. He
was one of those men who did not imagine
there was a really bad fellow living ; he had
seen so many, who had (as he would say) far
more good than harm in them, besides
knowing quite a host " of the best fellows on
earth."

His cousin Hamilton and he got on very
well together, though they were not very
similar in anything except looks, where they
had a strong resemblance; but Edmund
Hamilton was the better-looking, taller, and

slighter, with a more intelligent face. Hamilton was a far less free and independent member of society than Harry Lawson; he was the eldest son of a squire, whose property was in the same district as Lawson's; he had a sister and three brothers, and was of altogether of less importance in the social scale. The young men's mothers had been sisters, great *belles* of thirty years ago, and married to neighbouring county magnates.

Harry's mother had been many years dead, and his nearest relatives were the Hamiltons, with all of whom he was very intimate.

The young men walked home to The Grange, as the Hamiltons place was called. Harry had no objection to spending an eventhere; they were generally a gay party, Miss Hamilton, Harriet Hamilton, generally having some young girl staying with her, and being herself a **very** lively young lady; **she was** very good looking, just six-and-twenty, **with a most** vivacious manner, **a** good singer, **and** a still more practised flirt; **she was** the eldest of the family, and **it was the** great surprise of all those who first saw Harriet Hamilton that she had **not been** already married, and a subject **of far more** astonishment to herself. **Her** mother looked on the matter differently; she was not surprised, for she considered Harriet's manner and style as **not** at **all** calculated **to** attract; however, her opinion had **no** weight with her daughter.

Mrs. Hamilton **was a very** pleasing woman, **and one** could not **help admiring the** beauty which, after thirty years, **still** shone with some **of its old charm**; she had been more regularly **handsome than** her daughter, and she had other attractions, which her daughter **had not** inherited **from her.** She had a soft, low voice, a bright and pleasant smile. It was from her her son Edmund got his fine eyes; she had also a particularly good mouth, which he did not inherit, but with all her softness and her charms, few really cared for Mrs. Hamilton; she was always the same, always quiet, and low voiced, but her mind was centred on herself; husband, children, all else received but a very superficial attention from her; she cared for her husband as much, it may be more, than she cared for any one else. She was attached to her children, as she honestly believed, but she seldom thought of them; her greatest interest was in her daughter, and that was more the beauty's interest in her successor, in whom she recalled her own youth, than any more maternal passion; indeed, the word passion in no way applied to Mrs. Hamilton.

Harry was a favourite of his aunt; she at

all times expressed a regard for him; she, corresponded with him when he was away, hoped he would never become a wild young man, and gently scolded him with the same fascinating interest in his enormities which she had evinced in his father five-and-twenty years before.

And Harry loved his aunt better, perhaps, than any one else loved her; he paid her little attentions, brought her presents, wrote her long letters, and listened while she gently scolded him, and felt sure she was the image of his mother.

Mr. Hamilton was five-and-twenty years older than his wife, a very broken down, delicate old man, reserved, proud, and honourable, but one who took but little interest in the small social world around him. There were three younger brothers. Frederick, the second brother, was a young man of twenty, reading for the army, clever, and idle; the other two were boys at school, who were at present occupied with cricket and Latin, and counted as nobodies in the family circle.

When the young men reached The Grange, they found Mrs. Hamilton sitting over the drawing-room fire, in the dusky light of the November evening.

" Oh, how are you, Harry? Have you been long home?"

" Just come, aunt; and off again to-morrow."

" Oh! nonsense. Why would you go so soon? You are never at home."

" He is going up for his wedding, mamma; I was told so, I assure you, Harry."

" You are always hearing that identical piece of news of me, Harriet. What is the lady like, now?"

" Oh, hideous; a girl with a red nose, or

something equally dreadful; but do you know, we had a great ball down here since you left us."

" No, Edmund never told me."

"Oh! then Edmund danced a good deal with a certain young lady at it, I assure you."

" I can guess. Was she the belle? I forgot, my fair cousin, you were there, so I need not ask."

" They said a new belle had appeared, a blonde (Harriet was dark), a Miss Cavendish, just come from Paris, and staying with her sister."

" A new belle," said Harry. " How dreadful, Harriet; it was well I was not there ; I might have been taken captive. Oh! aunt ! you should have written me an account of this ball. Why, aunt is gone."

" Yes, papa is ill again ; she has gone to him, I think."

" Is he worse ?"

" Oh ! no, just the same."

" And was Ada Lowell at the ball ?"

" Oh ! of course ; and dressed in black, and sitting half the evening."

" No one asked her to dance, eh, Edmund ?"

" Oh ! Edmund of course made himself re-markable as usual."

" And Ada looked so pretty—did she though?" he said, turning to Edmund. " I know from the spite Harriet speaks with, how well she must have looked." And he laughed. " That's it, is it not, Harriet, dear ?"

Harriet found it rather difficult to look smiling still, as she said—

" So you may say, Harry. You did not see her; but she did though."

" And Edmund's so smitten, is he ?"

Edmund laughed, but the laugh was not

as good an attempt as some I have heard on
similar occasions. There was not enough of
pleased conceit in it to make it a good, dis-
claiming laugh. You would have inferred
that Edmund was one who had not as much
vanity as is allowable ; or that he was more
interested than he would have at all wished
to admit ; but he was not likely, one must
own, to make a good hypocrite. He had the
earnest-looking face, which could, I daresay,
feel a good deal ; the frank manner of one
unused to concealment. I do not think he
was very amiable, but I fancy he had, or
might have, the strong and concentrated
character which I fear is not so often united
to amiability ; for that which is so often
called amiability, is but a softness or weakness
of chararacter, a gentleness of heart, which
shrinks from paining another, though it yields
to one unworthy of the sacrifice. I fancy

Edmund had little of this; if his nature inclined him to be frank and earnest, it was also resolute and concentrated ; his frankness sprung, I think, more from a natural fearlessness of disposition than from a sociable character ; his attachments would be, I imagine, few; the influence of others over him small, for he was not yielding, and though gay and animated, he was not communicative.

If you could read his thoughts it was not from any wish on his part to submit them to your approval, but rather from his ignorance that they were more prominent than usual; he was quite capable of turning hypocrite, but as yet he had not seen the necessity.

Harriet and Harry made none of these reflections. Edmund's admiration of Ada Lowell was of secondary importance in her eyes, be it serious or not; and if Harry half suspected Edmund of being a little smitten, as he called it, he thought it a good subject for a quiz, that was all.

He was no fool, was Harry, on the contrary he had all that sense which is at a premium in the world; he knew he owned a good property, he knew he was good looking, and that he was considered a very good match, and his opinion of Harriet Hamilton was not at all lowered, rather, indeed, increased, by his knowledge that none of these advantages were lost on her; he thought with pleasure rather than otherwise, that she fully admitted his claims; he could see that she laughed at his jokes, pardoned his long absences, and quite forgave his never paying morning visits, evinced in fact in every way her appreciation of the future Mrs. Lawson's position, and was ready at any moment to accept it.

Mrs. Hamilton coming in, the conversation became general, and Harriet retired to make the most becoming toilet possible under the circumstances.

Mrs. Hamilton thought her nephew might one day or other become her son-in-law. She looked on at her daughter's manœuvres, and though she did not approve as a matter of taste, wished them success as a matter of policy. Harry brought his aunt in to dinner, and sat beside her. Harriet was his *vis-à-vis*, and they kept up a conversation all through dinner.

Old Mr. Hamilton was particularly lively, and told them stories of his younger days with a humour which showed, when his health permitted, what an agreeable companion he could be. He was a tall, thin man, gentleman like in appearance, little obtrusive of his ideas or wishes; those who knew him liked him, but over his own family he had little influence; his sons and he were not suited to each other;

too great a space of time separated them for
them ever to have been companions, and Mr.
Hamilton was of too reserved and abstracted
a mind to much influence young people; his
sons had never been in the habit of listening
to their father's opinions on any subject; in
some way, without apparent discussion, it
was settled the boys were to go into this or
that profession, and on Mrs. Hamilton de-
volved the measures for carrying it out; but
he could be exceedingly entertaining, from
his dry humour, and the acute observation
which you soon saw he possessed; he had seen
much of life, and he still retained the same
kindly feeling as in those early days, when he
and his old friend Crampton had travelled
through Asia together.

The dinner was over. Harriet's floating
pink had just disappeared, and Harry had to
himself admitted she looked " devilish well,"

when, as they re-assembled round the table, Edmund again asked Harry would he come to the meet at Sefton.

"What is to go on there?" Harry said. "It is a bad meet, a domain, not much chance of a run, unless the fox breaks for Corbetstown, and then it is all rocks. What makes you wish to go? Miss Lowell will be there, I suppose? I would have fancied that would have been a reason for wishing me away."

" Is that the lady I saw at lunch here some time since?" said Mr. Hamilton, to their surprise.

" Yes, sir," said Harry.

"A very nice girl," said the old gentleman.

" So Edmund thinks, sir," said Harry.

Mr. Hamilton began to laugh, Edmund to disclaim, and Fred and Harry to quiz, Fred suggesting " Edmund ought to go round by

Horton, and accompany Major Bethell. As they say he is engaged to her, you would be sure of a good reception, you know, Ned."

Hearing Harriet singing, Harry joined her in the drawing room, and spent the greater part of the evening turning over her music, while she, during the intervals between the songs, cross-questioned him as to all the places he had lately been at, and the young ladies he had flirted with; Harry protesting he never flirted when he was away from The Grange. It was a horrid habit he had learned from her, and quite foreign to his character; and his aunt scolded him for leaving again so soon, but as usual without an idea that he would change his plans in consequence of her doing so; in fact, she would have been embarrassed had he proposed anything of the kind.

CHAPTER II.

IT was a very fine hunting morning, the day of the meet at Sefton Hall ; soft and clear as some of those days in November sometimes are. There were some leaves still on the trees, and a great many berries on the hedge-rows; there had been rain the night before— soft, southern rain ; it still hung on the slender branches of the trees, though it was sunshiny and warm.

Any lady who ever went to see a meet of hounds would surely be out to-day, Edmund thought, as he rode Selim slowly down the old Grange avenue. The clouds still hung in heavy masses over the village outside the lodge gates; they were grey and lower than Edmund liked. He still though persisted in saying the lovely air, the soft southern breeze, would tempt anyone who ever thought of coming out.

He wondered as he rode along, was Ada Lowell dressing now; could it be that she had already determined not to join the meet. As these thoughts were passing through his mind, he heard a horse's foot behind him, and he had hardly passed from the shade of The Grange trees into the more open road, when he was overtaken by a fellow sportsman, whose arrival dispelled his reverie.

"Well, Hamilton, how are you old fellow? I think we are likely to have a good day; will you be in the first flight?"

"If I get a good start I shall try; but I think Selim will have a bad chance with Zoe. She seems in great condition to-day."

"I am afraid we are a little late," said Butler; "and Percy is always up to time. We may as well trot on; a morning like this he will be anxious to throw in the hounds at once."

They trotted on, and were not long in reaching Sefton. I will not say Edmund was delighted with his friend's company; however, they chatted most amicably, and Edmund contented himself with mental wishes for his absence.

Sefton Hall was a large domain, with fine old trees, and an immensity of cover; there was a rough hill side included in its extent, and from it the country sloped abruptly to the south. The house was large, old, and handsome; Mrs. Alton, the owner of Sefton

Hall, always gave a breakfast, and the meet
was a favourite one for those who wished
more to trot about and see their friends, than
ride, for there was not often a good run from
it.

Mrs. Alton was very particular that the
draw should not be a blank ; and it was seldom so, as the foxes had been well fed all the
summer by the gamekeeper, who knew his
mistress' fancy, and found Sefton a very
pleasant place, for with this exception, Mrs.
Alton allowed him to do very much as he
pleased; but her husband had been a fox-
hunter, and in her young days she often rode
to hounds. She still wished to see a cover
side drawn on a fine day, and recalled the
hours she had spent in the saddle with evident pleasure.

Her niece, Miss Lowell, was likely to be at
home Edmund thought; but he feared she

might have to accompany the old lady in her waggonette to the cover. He hoped some substitute might be found, and that Ada Lowell would be on horseback. Thinking of these probabilities, he rode with Butler up the long avenue, saw some waggonettes and phaetons already moving about, and a number of horsemen taking preliminary canters across the grass, with many of whom he exchanged the cordial greetings common to the hunting field. What an exhilarating scene! how productive of every kindly feeling is the meeting at a cover side! Who has not felt all his most generous feelings roused when hastening to the first meet of the season? He recognises in the happy faces round him companions who recall to his memory the pleasant recollections of many a gladsome run over hill and dale; of many a hazardous leap cleared by a **chance, which in less** exciting moments never would **have** been ventured on ; **of** that merry rivalry, which unlike almost every other kind of excitement, leaves but recollections which cheer **us** during life's many trials.

The master of the hounds and a considerable number of the field had gone into breakfast, and Edmund saw two or **three** ladies riding up and down. He rode on a little faster, but could not see his lady-love amongst **them.** Ada Lowell was doomed to the waggonette to-day he feared ; he rode up to the house. On the steps he met Major Bethill— **the** gentleman whom **his** brother Frederick had suggested was engaged **to** Miss Lowell ; they entered the house together, and soon met Mrs. Alton, who was dressed for driving, **and** who hoped they would have some sport.

" You are going to ride to-day, Mr. Hamilton?" said Mrs. Alton, turning to Hamilton,
who had just dispatched a glass of sherry.

" I'll try, Mrs. Alton," he said.

"Well, then," said she, "Major Bethill,
you are not going to ride, I hope; I want
some one to take care of my niece."

Bethill at once said he should be most
happy.

Miss Lowell came into the room almost at
this moment; her well-cut habit, tidy collar,
and perfect equipment, showed to advantage
a beautiful figure—tall, slight, supple; and
under her hat and veil shone such eyes,—
large, hazel, and beautiful beyond all other
eyes I have ever seen, in their ever varying
expression—now dark, now bright. The only
colour, as it seems to me, which equally ex-
presses tenderness and intellect; for blue is
peculiarly the eye of love, and black the eye

of intelligence: both are united in the ever varying hazel, which melts, and speaks, and flashes. Her hair was also peculiar in its richness and in its colour—a brown, mingled with a bright clear gold; otherwise her face was not remarkable; in complexion it was pale, and the features small.

"Major Bethill, Ada, says he will take care of you for me," said Mrs. Alton.

Miss Lowell thanked him, and said she would be ready at once.

Edmund, who had been standing in the window, advanced to shake hands. Ada said—

" I suppose you are going to ride to-day, Mr. Hamilton? I think, aunt, Mr. Percy has been waiting for you."

Mrs. Alton was sadly disconcerted by this information, and hurried off to the waggonette; Ada Lowell's horse was at the door, and

Hamilton left to Major Bethill the honour of assisting Mrs. Alton, that he might arrange Miss Lowell's bit.

"The chestnut looks very well, Miss Lowell," he said, as he fiddled with the bit.

" I think I can return Selim the same compliment," said she.

Major Bethill had mounted, the waggonette had passed on, and Edmund was still arranging Miss Lowell's bridle.

" We shall be late, Mr. Hamilton," she said.

Hamilton mounted; but to the old servant's disgust, the curb was found hanging half off, and had to be arranged ; he threw a glance of contempt at Hamilton, whom he looked at as a critic, on his mode of bridling a horse, and a most ignorant one—even Miss Lowell seemed to think his improvements not much to the purpose.

They at length trotted on briskly, and had but just come up to the gorse cover on the hill side, when the hounds gave cry.

" It is the old thing, in and out of the plantations on the hill side," said Bethill.

" Ride on, Major Bethill ; ride on, Mr. Hamilton ; you know I do not want an escort, I have old Thomas ; and I do believe we are going to have a run, I really think we are," she said, her eye brightening.

When he came out, Edmund was never less inclined to ride ; but since, it was evident there was no getting rid of Major Bethill, since he was not to have the pleasure of escorting Ada Lowell, he looked on the idea much more favourably.

The sharp note of the huntsman's " Gone away !" rang through the air ; a rush of excited horsemen passed them.

" They are gone over the hill," said Miss Lowell, riding on.

After a fast canter through two or three fields, there was a decided check in front ; and a " tally back," showed they had over-ridden the hounds.

" The fox has been headed, and is back to cover again," said Hamilton.

The fox, being a game one, did not dwell in the cover, and was now evidently breaking down hill for the open country. The hunts-man, having rapidly brought the hounds on the new line, the majority of the over-zealous were left in the rear, as the hounds, acknow-ledging the burning scent, rushed forward at full speed, their heads seldom touching the ground.

The hounds had raced through the first large grass field before the forward horsemen

were seen breaking from the cover side into
it.

Hamilton and Major Bethill had left Miss
Lowell, who had insisted on their not staying
with her. They took the first fence into the
grass field almost together, Hamilton remark-
ing, " It is likely to be a good thing." Through
the large field Hamilton's horse gained more
rapidly on the hounds, who were somewhat
checked by a high wall at the further end of
it. He tried to steady him coming to this
wall, but not being able to do so in time, the
horse bungled it, and both fell into the next
field. The major, having the possibilities
more in view, kept his mare better in hand ;
and steadying her on her haunches, put her
safely over it.

Hamilton was soon again in the saddle, and
on the line of the hounds, who had now settled
on their fox, and were descending the hill-side

through a scrubby and rocky country. In a few more strides, he came alongside Bethill. In the excitement of the moment, they both pressed forward on a line with the foremost hounds; the huntsman's " Hold hard! hold hard!" having very little power to restrain either of them.

The country became heavier, the fences more frequent. Hamilton's horse becoming steadier, made no second mistake, though both horses were beginning to show symptoms of distress; but Edmund was sorry to see the hounds pointing directly for the Goul — a stream which he had often crossed; but which was a serious obstacle to a half-tired horse, being bank full from the recent rains.

There was no time for swerving now, so Hamilton steadied Selim, and put him at the brook; the horse sprang forward boldly, but only landed with his forelegs on the opposite bank; Edmund sprang from the saddle, and they both succeeded in gaining footing on the bank, and were in the running again in an instant.

The major did not like the look of the brook; but fortune having favoured Hamilton, he could not bear to turn from it. He put his mare at it; she having a strong impression it was beyond her powers, resolutely refused, and to Bethill's chagrin, he saw Edmund again gaining on the hounds.

Bethill was still riding up and down, looking for an easier place to cross, when he was joined by a good many of the field. After a time, they all succeeded in crossing a little lower down, and on coming up with Hamilton, found him standing by a sewer where the fox had gone to ground.

Butler at once came up to Hamilton, enquiring for particulars of the run; he said that leaping through a quickset hedge, he had lost one of his stirrup leathers. "And did Bethill ride so well ? I should not have expected it," he said.

"He rode very well," said Edmund.

Edmund, from this day, began to consider Major Bethill's proceedings worthy of observation. As he rode home, he wondered, "had Ada Lowell seen any of the run ? Could she have recognised him ?" but on these points he asked his friend no questions.

Unfortunately, Ada had seen the performances of neither of these gentlemen ; she had ridden down a bye-road, expecting they would come back to the cover again in that direction, and had missed all ; her aunt had been more fortunate, and had seen a good deal of the riding. She highly applauded both Hamilton and the major,

" I think," she said, " Major Bethill would ride as well as Hamilton almost, if his mare was as good as Selim ; but my idea is that she is over-weighted."

CHAPTER III.

'REDERICK found his brother Edmund the
iorning after the hunt, contrary to his usual
ustom, sitting reading a book in a room
alled the study, which was particularly ap-
ropriated by Frederick and the younger
oys. Edmund sat there for some time, they
hatted on various subjects, then, of course,
ame the hunt, which he told over again, in-
roducing Major Bethill's name often, to see
Frederick would volunteer any information

about him, or admit how he heard, if heard he had, of his engagement; but Frederick preserved a discreet silence, having either forgotten all about the matter, or seeing the drift of his brother's conversation.

Finding it no use, Edmund gave it up, and walked out; but as he went along he could not help revolving the *on dits* in his mind. As he passed the study window he saw Frederick look up with a very mischievous expression of countenance; he turned into a walk further from the house, and consoled himself by imagining his brother was laughing at him.

" It is some of his confounded tricks from beginning to end," said he.

Still he could not dismiss the matter from his mind. What were Bethill's intentions— why did Mrs. Alton ask him to take care of Ada Lowell ?

Then he remembered Mrs. Alton had first asked him was he going to ride. Why did they ride against each other as they did if Bethill did not feel a secret rivalry also? and if Bethill was engaged to Ada would he leave her! He told himself that he would never have done so; he would not believe the Major was engaged to Ada—but he did believe him a most dangerous enemy. Had he ever seen Miss Lowell flirt with him?

He answered this by saying Miss Lowell was not a flirt; he could not recall to his mind any time at which she had flirted with him, though, he said, she must know I like her.

He wondered at the infatuation of women, and felt sure that she would marry Major Bethill merely because he was certain Bethill could not care for her one hundredth part as well as he would.

" And he is what they call good-looking, I
suppose," said poor Edmund, and he drew
himself up, and reflected how much bigger,
and heavier, and stronger he was; for Major
Bethill, though a plucky little fellow, was not
a fine-looking man like Hamilton, nor even,
in many women's eyes, as good-looking; but
Edmund loved his lady-love with that
nervous, anxious passion which never lets a
man see either his strong or his weak points.
If he met Ada out, and danced with her two
or three times, he at once concluded she loved
him—he was perfectly happy until the next
time they met, when her quiet manner and
cold reception showed him he had been
flattering himself in vain. Then Edmund
became jealous, and when jealous he was apt
to get into great huffs, and keep away from
his tormentor for days and weeks. Still he
said, walking up and down the laurel walk,

those had been happy days—those jealous fits had been but pettishness until now, when, for the first time, he really began to fear the future, and know what jealousy was. It sickened him to think, at this very moment, another might have robbed him of her; that quiet, cold manner with which she had ever met him, did it not show he had never touched her heart? she might, indeed, dance with him often of an evening, but what of that—had she not often said she liked dancing? and Edmund wondered how he could have considered that a compliment, and he was wretched, for he was in love, and he was jealous.

Do we not remember that happy time when we, too, were so miserable, when our hearts quickened, and our pulse beat at an allusion, a tone, a memory which brought before us the idol of our life; when our whole time was occupied, our minds filled with the one absorbing hope and idea, when all else seemed valueless and vain; if she was not to smile over our life's troubled sea we cared not how soon its waves closed over us. Yes, his heart too was glowing with that master passion, before which all of us mortals have bowed, some of us, aye, even to the dust, and bowed in vain.

And who was Ada Lowell? She was Mrs. Alton's niece and adopted daughter; she had come from India long ago to be brought up by her aunt, her mother being dead, and as Colonel Lowell was again married it was supposed she would never leave her aunt to rejoin him. Mrs. Alton said she hoped she would not; but Ada sometimes talked of her wish to see India for a year or so, a wish with which Edmund by no means sympathised.

When Edmund had reviewed all those possibilities, made himself as wretched as he could, and finished three or four cigars, he returned to the house, to find his brother Fred giving Harriet a slight sketch of his observations and suspicions concerning him, and could hear as he passed Harriet's laugh at the perfect fool Edmund did make of himself; Fred good-humoredly adding, " Well, she is a nice girl though, Harriet ; but *you* see if she is not married to Bethill, that's all."

Shortly afterwards Harriet drove out in her little pony phaeton ; she went to the barracks at Horetown to see some ladies, wives of the officers, whom she knew, and more especially to hear the gossip of the day, which Harriet always provided herself with liberally. She heard what a good run they had had from Sefton, how very unfortunate Major Bethill was in not getting his horse over the stream; but she did not hear that he had been much at

Sefton lately, nor if he was going to be married to Miss Lowell. She then told her friend, the wife of Captain Cole, that she had heard Major Bethill was a great admirer of Ada Lowell; but she could elicit nothing from Mrs. Cole, who was merely cynical, and said "for her part she greatly doubted Major Bethill's admiring any young lady, at least, seriously," but gave Harriet no facts, and was therefore, in Harriet's opinion, not very well worth listening to.

Having discovered nothing that she was anxious about, Harriet set out on her way home, stopping to flirt with a few young ensigns *en passant* as she drove through the town—young gentlemen who, from her condescension, concluded they had undoubtedly captivated her, and that at any moment they were weak enough to encourage such feelings on her part she would accept their hand and name, and follow the fortunes of the 129th, as Mrs. Cole and Co. did.

Harriet's ideas of life were, however, somewhat different, and at present were directed towards securing, by some means or other, Harry Lawson, whose being about four years younger than she, was, in her eyes, a point which made the matter more feasible: in fact, he was, perhaps, even now too old for her views in some respects.

On her return from her drive, she gave her mother a history of her proceedings, telling her her own ideas, and Frederick's, on the subject of Edmund and his love affairs. Mrs. Hamilton listened with her gentle, pleased expression, gave no opinion as to whether she agreed or not with those ideas, expressed a wild curiosity as to Major Bethill's love affair, "if love affair it was;" but none whatever as to her son's, except that "if it were

true, it would **indeed** be so like Edmund."
Miss Hamilton, however, was accustomed to
her mother's manner, **and** did not consider
there was much **reason** to doubt she would in
all things oppose her son's choice, though she
received the intelligence with such apparent
unconcern.

" Mamma," said Harriet, abruptly, " I want
you to give a ball."

" A ball ! dear Harriet," said Mrs. Hamilton ; " how foolish !"

" Why foolish, mamma? every one gives
balls."

" But, Harriet, if you and Fred are right
in your suspicions, I think it would be very
foolish."

" Oh! he can see Ada Lowell any where, if
he cares ; but I cannot see Harry every day."

" Harriet, dear, do not speak in that way,
it pains me really to hear you."

" Oh, stuff, mother, you know as well as I what a good thing it would be for me—and how am I to captivate Harry if I don't see him ?"

" He can come here, you know, dear."

" Oh, nonsense! mother; you know he will not come here. What use is there in talking in that way ?"

" Harriet," said her mother, sitting up in her chair, and speaking quite fast for her, " you know if Harry wishes to see you, he can come; I do not believe any girl succeeds better by hunting young men."

Although Mrs. Hamilton condescended to use the argument of expediency, it was evident from the glow on her cheek she was humiliated by her daughter's sentiments; for though worldly, Mrs. Hamilton was proud— and proud women consider such plotting mean, when the victim of it has shewn no preference for the girl; if he has they seem to agree that a few steps in advance on her part are only injudicious, not contemptible.

Harriet, who was quite incapable of taking her mother's views, said—

" I am sure it is very unkind of you, you do not seem to care at all about me."

" As to giving the ball, I shall do that I am sure," said Mrs. Hamilton ; " but you see, if I do, it brings Ada Lowell and Edmund together ; if he asks her, your father will not object, and then he will, I am almost sure, assent to a good settlement on Edmund, and that will be a bad thing for you all; and if Edmund is married, you will not be asked out as much as you have been."

"That has been of much good to me, mamma !"

" But, my dear, you will find it will have an effect, you will, indeed ; still, I am sure,"

she said, her old suave manner returning,
" why should I not wish Edmund married
and happy ?   I do hope he may be so : he is
a very nice young man, and has been such a
good son."

Mrs. Hamilton spoke these words in her
usual gentle, pleading tone, and I must say, I
fear, attached no meaning whatever to them ;
if any, it was, " If you, Harriet, choose to run
the risk of getting your brother married, why
then it is quite a matter of indifference to
me."

Harriet, who knew her mother well, met
this by saying—

" Just so, mother, so let us have the ball—
as you say, Edmund cannot be helped, I suppose he will marry her if she will have him :
it is little matter whether it is sooner or later,
but do let us have the ball."

" Well, dear, as you wish it so, I shall try.

I hope your father's health will not interfere; but he seems better of late, don't you think so ?"

" He is as well as usual," said Harriet, and taking up her hat she walked out of the room.

" What a strange girl she is !" Mrs. Hamilton thought. " I cannot understand her, and she does such queer things. I wish, I do wish, she was married; but how can I expect she will marry well ! It is a great pity she has such a bad manner—for she is certainly very handsome, every one says so—and it is so painful to see her go on as she does.'

Mrs. Hamilton's ideas then reverted to the contemplated ball, and in thinking what dress she would wear, she happily forgot her son's infatuation, and her daughter's self-will.

CHAPTER IV.

EDMUND heard with pleasure of the ball; he hoped, then, at least, to discover whether these rumours were, or were not, well-founded. In the meanwhile, the days passed slowly, very slowly; the walks by the laurel hedge were getting longer and longer; and yet his ideas were not clearer as to the real state of affairs. He often resolved he would go over and see Ada Lowell, and again he remembered he was not in the habit of paying visits at Sefton, and concluded it was better to wait for the night of the ball.

He was roused from this state of mind by
receiving an invitation from Major Bethill to
dine at the mess at Horetown.   He thought
it strange,—their acquaintance had been but
slight, the Major had dined at the Grange
once or twice, but it was some time ago,
and they had since seen but little of each
other until the day of the hunt.   Was Bethill
also anxious to see and judge for himself the
man whom he had ridden against? did a secret
rivalry sharpen his curiosity also?   Edmund
doubted whether he would go—yet his great
desire to know better what this man was like,
who was, perhaps, preferred to him, decided
him;—he would go and see, and try to divine
the future before his idol, if she had already
given it into Bethill's keeping.   That he
might be prejudiced and unable to decide the
point justly, he never thought of for a moment ; at times he even fancied he should

feel glad for her sake to find Bethill all that she deserved, but the notion was hateful to him. He would not even admit that Bethill might be attached to Ada. He remembered she was said to have a large fortune from her aunt, and that alone was the attraction in the Major's eye, he felt confident. "He must be near forty—how could he love her? he has had many love affairs before this," muttered Edmund, who, absorbed in life's first passionate hopes, had little sympathy with the mature and well-weighed preferences of middle life.

Hamilton was very cordially received at Horetown Barracks by Major Bethill, who was in temporary command. There were not many present at mess, it being leave season; they were principally young men from different regiments who were congregated at the depôt battalion.

When dinner was half over, Major Bethill, turning to Capt. Cole, who sat near him, said—

"Did you take a look at Pioneer, to-day?"

"I did not; I was about town all day, but I told young Crampton; he said he'd go."

"Crampton! where is he?" said Bethill.

"I think," said a pale-faced man they called Gaynor, "he is dining out; but I was down seeing the horse cantered with him."

"How did he go?"

"Very well; the jock said he was improving rapidly, but Crampton and I thought he was drawn a little too fine."

"'Pon my soul, Gaynor, that Crampton knows nothing about a horse; he lost the Maidstone cup all through being fattened up, till—I give you my word—" said Bethill, turning to Hamilton, "he was more pig than racer."

"I think," said Cole, "Johnstone does not ride him well; pulls him about too much, eh, Major?"

"Not at all; no better man than Johnstone. He will take him through it well, if any man can; 'pon my honour, I can't be everywhere. Some of you fellows should look after him."

"What is he entered for?" asked Hamilton.

"The County Plate; he is light weighted, from our last ill-luck; so he ought to be sure of it."

"A strong horse only can win that," said Hamilton.

"I wish," said Bethill, "you would give us your opinion, Hamilton. You can ride a horse; so I suppose you know how he ought to be treated. He is a very good looking

animal; I picked him up for a mere trifle—
only two hundred and fifty pounds; I give
you my word. We have shares in him; it
just gives one an interest in a race, having
something to say to the horses, don't you
think so?"

A young man from the end of the table
said—

"I'll sell my share to anyone who wants
it. I don't think he will turn out anything;
in my mind he is a coarse looking brute."

"Coarse brute," said the Major, overhear-
ing, "and Gaynor and Crampton say he is
too fine drawn; did you ever hear such
stuff? I must look up Johnstone; I hope he
is not beginning to smell a rat, as he would,
if he saw too much of Crampton; those
jockey fellows, sir, see through you at a
glance, and if they think you are not up to
them, they will lead you a pretty dance."

" Has the jock any interest in winning ?"
said Edmund.

" Of course, my good sir," said the Major;
" leave an old soldier alone for that. He is
concerned in the event himself; I saw to
that."

The young man, who had said he was a
worthless brute, turning to Gaynor, said—

" I intend hedging, if I get the chance;
take my advice, and try what you can do in
that line."

The Major seemed greatly annoyed by this
observation.

" D—— me, I can't see what you fellows
are at," he said. " You have a splendid animal, and you are blowing on him yourselves;
do you all want to hedge? Hang me, if I'll
trouble myself again to buy a good thing."

Cole, who saw that Bethill was getting a
little angry, and who was a good humoured

creature, always trying to preserve peace at any price, now proposed a game of cards. Edmund assented, and the Major, Cole, Gaynor, and he sat down. Major Bethill seemed pleased ; he and Cole were partners, and Gaynor and he had soon several bets on the colour of the cards as they turned up, the odd trick, &c.

" Did you meet Miss Lowell on your way home ? " Bethill said to Hamilton. " You have lost again, Gaynor—Gad ! we treated her somewhat unceremoniously ; I wonder what became of her ?"

" I did not meet her afterwards," said Hamilton.

" She was furious, I am convinced," said Bethill, laughing.

Edmund laughed too.

" A very pretty girl," said the Major, " very, 'pon my word; quite a style about

her, and a great catch! Thirty thousand
they say; she has good reason to toss her
head at every fellow she meets."

Hamilton could not say that was exactly
one of Ada Lowell's characteristics; but it
seemed to be a matter of course in the owner
of thirty thousand pounds in Major Bethill's
eyes.

"She may not get a shilling though, I
understand, if she does not please the old
lady," he said, enquiringly.

"Yes, I believe so," said Hamilton; " her
father could give her nothing, you know."

" I suppose the old dame is looking out for
a sprig of nobility. You should ask your
cousin down here, Gaynor."

"Oh! Fitzallan," said Gaynor; " yes, it
would suit him, with a title and not a penny."

" Could we pawn you off for him? Eh,
Gaynor? That would give you a lift.

This Gaynor was a strange looking creature—a mere school boy; he had a painful
habit of colouring when anyone spoke to him.
He seemed to be an established butt, and
there was a nervous expression in his face
very disagreeable to meet; he had evidently
been betting far more than he could afford to
lose, and his face, as the cards turned up, was
a sight to see. The Major and Captain Cole
were quite masters of their countenances, and
in no way could you guess their fortune from
their faces.

Mr. Gaynor being called for something,
left the room.

"Did you ever see such a being?" said
Bethill; "but we will not be troubled with
him long. I can foresee that; and the young
ass bets as if he were a millionaire."

Bethill, himself, seemed in no way indis-
posed to bet in what he called moderation.

Hamilton, who seldom played, was surprised
at the sums staked around him; and although
the best able to bear the loss, he could not
help being provoked to see poor Gaynor, who
had resumed his seat, more wild than ever in
his play; when fortune seemed deserting him,
then apparently, according to Gaynor, was
the time to double the stakes, and so, I presume, win back the flying goddess. At last
from bets on the cards, as they turned up,
stakes, and so forth, Gaynor must have lost
fully a hundred pounds; this seemed to quite
stupefy him. Major Bethill said something
about his making way for some one else, if
he did not care to risk anything further, and
Hamilton took advantage of the change to
say he would leave them also; and Gaynor,
calling for brandy and soda, sought the common refuge of the unlucky.

When the party broke up Edmund, too, had lost considerably, and Major Bethill was the largest winner. As Hamilton left the ante-room he was much struck with Gaynor's face, which had a more wretchedly nervous expression than ever. Captain Cole, who had won a good deal from him, was proposing they should have another chance for it all. Gaynor seemed inclined to consent, but Bethill interfered.

" Gaynor had better play no more to-night," said he. " You should let him alone, Cole. Don't you see," he said, turning to Hamilton, " he hardly knows where he is ?"

Hamilton thought he certainly did not know much more. He could not help pitying the wretched boy, who was so totally unfit for the life he had embarked on.

" Who is he ?" said he, to Captain Cole.

" He is related to the Fitzallans, who have

always taken care of him," said Cole; " he
has no father or mother, and hardly any
money. They got him his commission for
nothing, but they might have saved themselves
the trouble."

" He talked of his Cousin Fitzallan."

" Yes, just so ; heir to a title and nothing
a year; but he is not like Gaynor, he is a
deuced sharp fellow."

" Good-night, Hamilton."

" Good-night, Major."

And Edmund was on his way home, his
convictions as to Bethill's character not much
altered, except that he admitted that he was
an agreeable man, and had a manner which
could hardly fail to please and amuse when
so inclined; but Edmund saw that at all times
he did not employ it; and he fancied that to
such fellows as Gaynor he could make himself almost insupportable, from the jeering,

patronising tone he assumed, and the way in which he would attract universal attention to their peculiarities. He thought of his own brother, and wondered how he would get on with his love of excitement and dislike to control; but these matters were dismissed from his mind by at length finding himself at home, and observing it was already past four.

CHAPTER V.

THE evening of The Grange ball had arrived. It was to be a large affair. Mr. Hamilton was not more unwell than usual, but he protested he would not stay up for supper.

Harriet had taken especial trouble with her toilet. She was dressed in a soft shade of pink crape, I think; her hair was a work of art, and when flowers and pearls had been added in profusion she felt confident she looked her very best, and the feeling deepened her colour, and gave greater confidence to her

bearing. Her mother, in a handsome dress
of some dark material, enveloped in costly
laces, was still an interesting and pleasing
woman ; but a nervous look in her eyes when
she saw Harriet showed she had not confidence enough in her daughter to feel satisfied
at her appearance.

"I think your dress very pretty, and in
good taste, Harriet," she said.

"Well, mamma, so will Harry, I hope,"
Harriet answered, seeing clearly the expression I have alluded to in her mother's eye.

"There will be a great many here. Do
not make yourself remarkable," Mrs. Hamilton said.

"Oh! it is only while people are here
that it is worth while being remarkable,"
Harriet said, as she swept out of the room to
take a survey of the whole establishment and
see all was right, for she was a very efficient

manager of household affairs, and things were seldom at fault that came under her control, and her mother, who cared little for such matters, had partially abdicated in her favour.

The first two or three dances were over, the guests had all arrived, the rooms were very much crowded, and it began to be whispered about that the belle of the evening was a pretty Miss Cavendish, who had just come from Paris on a visit to a sister, who lived in a neighbouring county. She was an exceedingly pretty blonde indeed, and Harry Lawson had already danced with her twice.

Edmund had been dancing with one or two young ladies, whose claims could not be ignored, but he was engaged to Ada Lowell for the next gallop.

"How very well Miss Lowell is looking," said Mrs. Hamilton to a lady who sat beside her, and who, having no daughters of her own, impartially admitted it was so.

"She is indeed. I do not wonder that gentlemen admire her. I think her face so attractive. Your own daughter, too, is looking very well; so old Colonel Travers thinks, I am sure."

Mrs Hamilton glanced at Harriet, who was talking with great animation to her companion. There was rather a dissatisfied look on her face, which her mother was pained to see. She instinctively glanced round to observe if Harry was in the room; he was not to be seen, but shortly after he passed through to the conservatory, with Miss Cavendish on his arm; he was paying her, apparently, great attention, and she seemed to listen with a pleased and flattered expression. Mrs. Hamilton also watched Ada Lowell with particular attention. Ada had not as yet danced with either Major Bethill or Edmund; but Harriet, following her mother's instructions, had expressly brought Major Bethill to her, that she might talk to him, for Mrs. Hamilton said she had quite forgotten him. Almost at the same time, Harriet introduced Colonel Travers to her mother, and after a few words only on Major Bethill's part, he and Harriet left for the dancing room.

Colonel Travers, a stately-looking, grey haired old man, exerted himself to please Mrs. Hamilton, and with success; for while her own claims to please lay in her apparent gentleness and cordiality, she rather liked in others a certain mannerism, which he possessed.

Edmund and Ada were dancing; he had asked her—

" If she forgave him for leaving her the day of the hunt at Sefton ?"

" Forgave you ; why you had nothing to do with taking care of me, Mr. Hamilton. Major Bethill was to do so, according to my aunt."

" But, perhaps, but for my bad example, Major Bethill might not have deserted you."

" You think Major Bethill very easily led away. Did I not ask both of you to leave me, and ride on ?"

" In his place, I should not have gone."

" But you did go."

" I was not in his place," said Edmund.

" You both left me, and joined the hunt," persisted Miss Lowell.

" See what it is to take a lady at her word ; you are angry that I went."

" I am not the least angry, except," she said,

her face slightly flushing—"except for your saying I did not want you to take me at my word. You have no reason to say any such thing."

"I see you have not forgiven me for leading away Major Bethill."

Ada Lowell, beginning to suspect that Edmund was jealous of the Major, which she had not till then imagined, her face again flushed, and her beautiful expressive eyes dilated.

"Confess it was very wrong," she said.

"After all you said, you admit you were angry on his account."

There was a bitter tone in Edmund's voice as he said this, which annoyed Ada, who had been up to this quite good humoured; her face changed with a rapidity which showed she could not be lectured with impunity.

"I do not see why I need admit anything;

have I given you any right to lecture me, Mr. Hamilton ?"

She looked better as she spoke than Edmund had ever seen her look, with a slight flush on her pale cheek, and those eyes which made her peculiar beauty struggling to anticipate her lips, and say how angry she was. Yet it was that gentle, womanly anger which you could not like her less for, for it sprung from her sensitive woman's pride.

Edmund's admiration shone in his eyes so unmistakably, that before them Ada's sank ; the angry brilliancy suffused into softness, the slight flush rose into a deeper hue ; Edmund stopped in the dance mechanically.

" You don't think—you must know why I seem rude," he said.

" I do not wish to know anything more about it, Mr. Hamilton ; let us not speak of it ; and now please bring me to my aunt."

Edmund tried to say something, but Ada stopped him.

"Now do not speak again," she said. " Aunt is up at the upper end of the room, and I am engaged to Major Bethill for the next."

Edmund said no more. She sat down beside her aunt, with whom, for a few moments, he conversed.

" This is our dance, Miss Lowell," said Major Bethill, coming up.

" Yes," Ada said, "I believe so."

" It is the dance of the evening to me."

Edmund did not hear Miss Lowell's reply, but she laughed lightly, and they were soon whirling round. Bethill danced very well; he was about five feet ten, his figure was slight and youthful, and as they passed, Hamilton admitted that there was no apparent disparity in years, and that Bethill was a tolerably handsome man. It is, he thought, his character, his view of things, which makes him old, which makes him unsuited to her; sensitive and romantic as she is, she will picture him all she would admire, and if she only heard how he talked of her and her money!

Harriet came up.

"Edmund," she said, "do dance with Kate Blackall; she ought to receive some attention; she is there near the large window."

Edmund went over and asked her; she at once assented for the next galop; she was a pretty little girl.

"Oh! I am so fond of dancing, Mr. Hamilton, are you?"

"Yes, sometimes; yes, certainly, with a good partner, as I have at present."

"No," she said, "you don't care much for dancing, I can see that."

"I have been dancing longer than you have been, Miss Blackall."

"Yes, you danced a long time with Miss Lowell; you were dancing with her when we came."

"I meant I have been dancing for some years before you ; you won't care for it so much in five years. I have been dancing for five years, while you were playing with your dolls."

" Does Miss Lowell dance very well?"

" Yes, very well, as well as you do."

" You don't think that ; you know you like dancing with her best."

" You say that just because I did not ask you first," said Edmund, not caring much what he said to so very exigeant a young lady.

" I say it, and it is true—quite true, is it not ?"

Edward, who was half distracted by this line of conversation, said—

" How can you say so?"

" Where is your card? There, let me see it; how many dances are you engaged to Miss Lowell for?"

" Have you one after supper to spare me?" he said, which happily, for the moment stopped her inquiries, and Edmund thought he would begin; so he said, " Do you think Major Bethill a good dancer?"

"I have not danced with him; I don't know him, but I have just seen him dancing with Miss Lowell. Are they to be married?"

" I don't know; yes, I have heard so."

" You are vexed; yes, now really I see it, you are jealous."

" Was there ever such an intolerable girl," thought Edmund. " How she does worry one. Why don't you sometimes drive to see the hounds meet, or ride there, Miss Blackall ?"

"Oh, papa won't let us ; he says it is no place for ladies," said the retiring Kate ; "gentlemen are tormented with them."

"Do you believe it, Miss Blackall?"

"Oh ! indeed, yes ; you know, that if there is a run, papa says ladies are quite in the way; they keep gentlemen with them, and then accidents happen to them."

"Happen who ?"

"The ladies, of course ; and papa does not approve, you know."

"I am sorry he does not; I should have thought a hat would have been very becoming to you," he said, gravely, as the dance being over, he released himself from his tormenter, who reminded him when leaving her of the after supper dance.

As Edmund walked into the next room, he saw his cousin Harry and Miss Cavendish sitting in the library talking very earnestly—Harry, taken captive by the new face, as usual. Passing his mother, she said—

" Have you danced with Miss Cavendish? They tell me she is the belle here to-night."

" No, mother, I would not for the world; it would be treating Harry badly."

" Oh, does Harry admire her?"

" Yes, he is quite in love; it is an established fact now."

" Why, did he meet her before?"

" Oh, an age ago, mother," Edmund said, just to get rid of the subject; but Mrs. Hamilton told her daughter, when she next saw her, that Edmund had said Miss Cavendish was an old flame of Harry's; he had known her some time.

" Oh," said Harriet, " but mamma, did you

like my conquest; I am afraid you have taken him from me, a gay widower, with a daughter as old as I am almost. Don't laugh, you will see me a stepmother very soon; but I must make Fred dance ; he is very provoking."

Edmund walked into the conservatory. Harry and his partner had joined the dancers; he sat down in the window at the end of it. He was looking out of the curtains into the lighted room beyond, when his eye caught Miss Lowell's dress ; from the shadow where he sat, he could see clearly, but they could not see him. Major Bethill was asking her—

" Was she nervous left by herself the other day. 'Pon my word," he said "after I had gone a field or two, I began to think of you, and how I had treated you ; and I felt so disgusted with myself. I did not much care about the run, or how I rode; it was easy for Hamilton, whose whole heart was in it, to beat me."

"I believe you rode very well notwithstanding," Ada said.

"I was beat at a stream by Hamilton; he is a good horseman, and cares for nothing so much as riding; how I like that in a young fellow—it shows determination; I like a fellow to ride like that."

"Yes, I believe he rides very well."

"Remarkably well, and there is nothing I like better, it shows such pluck, and Hamilton is a very determined fellow; you see that at a glance. I like the way he plays, too."

He paused for Miss Lowell to ask a question, but she said nothing.

"One can see a man's character," he added, musingly, "even in a game of cards; the way a man bets, the way a man loses. Now, I never saw a man who loses so coolly as Hamilton; I'll give you my honour he and Gaynor lost near a hundred-and-fifty the other night, and it might be sixpence the way Hamilton took it; as to poor Gaynor, if you could see the way he got on, howling over his money, and his friends."

" Did he lose much ?" said Miss Lowell.

The tone of her voice pained Edmund very much as he overheard her.

" Well, yes for him—yes, but not much; but I should not talk of these things, I would not to any one but you; but you, dear Miss Lowell, know that men in my position must see a good deal of this kind of thing. I take a hand myself often," he said, " as I can hardly well escape doing so, you know, and I have to take care of myself," and he laughed gently. " You seemed chilled; let us not

stand here, there are drafts about these windows, and glass."

"I do not feel it; it only seems to me fresh
and pleasant;" and she sat down on a low
chair.

Edmund felt wretched; he would appear a
listener if he moved, and any one, by opening
the other door, and throwing the light on his
seat in the recess, would at once disclose his
position; he saw Ada's white dress; he could
see the gleams of lights on the back of her
hair, and the string of gold coins on it; her
face was in shadow, she was slowly moving
her fan. He could see the Major standing
further from him, just at her shoulder, and he
knew that he was speaking, but it was so fast
and low he could not hear a word; the fan
moved slowly back and forwards—it stopped
—she looked up, and spoke quickly, and at
length, but he could not hear; the Major

seemed to repeat some assertion, at least, from his gestures he inferred it to be so, and Ada got up and walked into the light, followed by Bethill.

Edmund was furious; he now saw, was positive, he thought, that Bethill was her lover, and might he not be equally sure he was not very coldly received. Why did she sit there and listen to that long earnest conversation; it was plain it was not interrupted by her. Edmund's rage reminded him how necessary it was to make an effort to conceal it; he hurried into the dancing-room, and soon found a partner, and danced incessantly until supper time; at supper he found himself not far from Kate Blackall.

" You have forgotten our dance, I know you have," she said.

He went over to her side; he was in the humour to flirt with her—to do anything disagreeable and hateful, so that it did not give him time to think.

" I have not forgotten. Pray come now ! "

They passed near Ada Lowell, and Kate laughed gaily just then.

" Did you see Miss Lowell looking at us? you will be scolded for this, I am afraid."

" You want to torment me, Kate—Miss Blackall, I mean."

They were near Ada. Did he wish to be overheard?

" You should not call me Kate; Miss Lowell would not like it."

" Do you like it ? " said Hamilton ; " that seems to me more to the purpose."

" How can you say such things? but you know—that is, of course, yes—no."

" Then I shall call you Kate."

" Oh no; it would not be right, and Miss

Lowell would be angry, and it would be thought strange."

And she blushed, and looked confused, hanging her head, and looking very pretty. And Edmund, who well knew how silly and forward she was, forgot it in her prettiness and his rage.

"And Ada Lowell ?" she said, as they stopped dancing close to the spot where Ada had sat.

As she said " Ada," she threw down her eyes and looked so demure.

Edmund laughed.

She certainly was a great little flirt; but that only the more suited him in his present mood. As they stood chatting Miss Lowell passed them ; she looked across—there was a strange expression in her speaking eyes—a sad questioning look. Edmund saw it; it was not jealousy or pique, it was sadder, and and at the same time calmer.

"Does she no longer care to seem angry with me?" he thought, and he soon disengaged himself from Kate's slight meshes, intending to observe further, but he found Ada and her aunt had left. Feeling the influence her presence still had over him, he thought "What a fool I have been! Now, if Kate Blackall was to die for me I doubt very much whether I should pity her. Not that she would die for anyone; but is it so with Ada, does she not care if I die for her?" He recalled her blush, and his mind wandered off to the points in which she differed from Kate Blackall.

He stood in the library thinking, when his mother passed by him. She saw his attitude, the expression of his eyes, and, although she had little affection for her son, she felt sympathy for the lover—his face, for the moment, recalled the memory of one who had loved her well: she, for the time, forgot her worldliness, but only for the time.

" Edmund, dear, you look tired," she said, and putting out her hand she gently stroked his shoulder.

" Yes, a little, mother,' he said.

And she passed on, but Edmund often thought of her kind glance — her slight caress.

CHAPTER VI.

Harriet came into her mother's room the morning after the ball. It was nearly two o'clock, but Mrs. Hamilton had not yet breakfasted.

"I hope you are not very much tired," she said.

"My head does ache so, Harriet, dear."

"I hope papa is not complaining much. He did not stay up long."

"Not worse, I think, but he says that late hours are most injurious to him."

"Did you like everything, mother?"

"Yes, I thought everything went off very well."

"Did you see Harry, mother?"

"I did—he was very much taken up with Miss Cavendish."

"Yes," said Harriet, "taken up indeed; she is very pretty, is she not?"

"Well, Harriet, dear, I daresay gentlemen think so—she seems admired; I have seen many I thought more attractive; but she is pretty."

"I might marry Colonel Travers, if I liked," said Harriet. "What would you think of that, mother?"

"Are you serious about it, dear? he seems so much older than you are, and he has a daughter so grown up."

"I am serious enough after last evening; you can see what a chance I have of Harry;

I won't forget that," she said, her brow lowering.

" Oh, he is just caught for the moment, perhaps."

" He is never a moment he is not caught with some one or other ; besides it's too dangerous to refuse Colonel Travers. I never had as good a chance."

" Why, has he proposed for you? you have not seen much of him, have you ?"

" Yes, I have at Brighton with aunt last summer. Yes, he has proposed for me, and I said I would write to-day."

" Oh, dear, Harriet, it is so sudden, and why did you never speak of it before—why, you were always talking of Harry."

" Of course I would have Harry if I had a chance."

" Well, dear, perhaps, as you say yourself, there never was much prospect of that."

" Prospect !" said Harriet, fiercely, " I was sure of him but for that hateful girl, and I will be revenged yet."

" Oh, Harriet, that is folly; women never can be revenged on the men they care for; you cannot be revenged on Harry without being disgraced."

" I both will and can. Why can't women be revenged as well as men ?"

" You know, dear, how foolish all this is." —Harriet made an impatient gesture.—" But are you serious about Colonel Travers?" said Mrs. Hamilton, who was beginning to think it was all pique on Harriet's part.

" Well, yes, mother, I am; what better can I do—he will be able to make a comfortable settlement on me, as I have heard he is very well off. He certainly has two children, the daughter you know, and a son in a regiment in Canada. I suppose it is the very best thing I can do."

This way of speaking quite put Mrs. Hamilton out, she would have approached the subject so differently; she was, however— now the first shock of intelligence was over— much more reconciled to the prospect, in fact any prospect of getting Harriet married was not without its charms.

" In a worldly point of view, it would be a good match," said she, blandly. " He is older than you are, much older: I myself married a man five-and-twenty years older than I was, so I should not speak of that."

" He is just sixty," said Harriet.

Her mother did not contest the point, she merely said—

" Yes—of course no one could object to such a match ; your father or brothers, I mean."

"I don't agree with you, they will all object more or less; but what is that, they can't prevent my doing what I please—but I should rather they did not," Harriet added, more gently, "it might provoke Colonel Travers, and who would see about the settlements."

Harriet was then silent, and after a pause her mother said—

"I shall arrange it first with your father, and then all will be right; and I do hope and pray that it may be for your welfare, Harriet, dear, as I am sure it is."

"You are more sanguine than I am then, mother. I only know it's the best thing for me to do, since I have lost Harry: but I will be revenged, I will not let him off so easily."

"My dear, be cautious, you cannot be revenged; why talk of it, why think of it?"

"What else can I think of? can I forget

that it has been talked of over the whole country that I was to be married to Harry?"

"Well, it has ; but the best thing that you can do now is to marry some one else. I speak in this way because it seems to me there has been no foundation for all the talk there has been ; if you tell me there has, I will say nothing."

"He has flirted with me, nothing more," Harriet said, with unwilling truth.

"Then, my dear, I seldom speak ; but if you go on in this way, you will make yourself ridiculous. Are not all women who exhibit any preference, which is not returned, ridiculous?"

"What right had he to flirt with me, to give rise to these reports?"

"As to all this, it seems to me to be perfect folly. Harry has never asked you to marry him—he need not have been afraid of a refusal," said Mrs. Hamilton, with some humour. "So I presume he must have been deterred by the fear of your accepting him, eh?"

Harriet's hard face flushed at this insult, but her mother knew her well, it was the only way to rule that callous nature.

"Therefore, my dear," she said, "take my advice, and make a good match when you can—that is, if you, like most girls, care for being married. If you do not marry, you don't know what may occur; and if it is a thing this affair of yours with Colonel Travers should be spoken of, how very injurious to have it, too, broken off."

Mrs. Hamilton spoke vaguely to alarm her daughter, if possible, in the only way she could be alarmed.

"And what," said Harriet, with one of her startling transitions, "what did you think of Edmund?"

"I think you and Fred are right. I did not see much of Fred—was he dancing?"

"He did dance —and he is right, you think ? Will she have Edmund, do you think, mother ?"

" I hope so, dear," said her mother, slyly; " if you are married, I should greatly wish to have Edmund settled, and why not with her ?"

Harriet doubted the genuineness of her mother's wishes, but said nothing, not caring to pursue the subject, when she knew she would elicit nothing.

" He will be angry about my marriage, I am sure," she then remarked.

"You will leave me to tell him, I hope, Harriet ; it will be better."

"I am too abrupt, you think—well, per-haps I am. Do you think I have any chance of Harry ?"

" Harry !" her mother said, startled at this return to him, at a time she had begun to order the wedding breakfast in imagination. " I do not,—I cannot say I do."

" I will be revenged, then, that's all," said Harriet, walking away.

Mrs. Hamilton could not help thinking over the character of the daughter she was so soon perhaps to lose. She wondered how, as a step-mother, she would get on with Colonel Travers' children ; what sort of man he was. She thought, with dread, of her remaining unmarried; the strange things she had already done, the stranger she would be likely to do in this matter. " I must try," she thought, " and get her father to assent at once, however I manage it; she would be more unmanageable than ever if I failed; and this mad talking of being revenged on Harry, she will be occupied about the wedding, and will forget it all I suppose."

Mrs. Hamilton lost no time in approaching the subject **with** her husband : she said Harriet had been talking to her of a proposal she had just received, and she imagined from the way she spoke she had made up her mind to marry.

" **Who is** it ?" said Mr. Hamilton.

" **Old** Colonel Travers," said his wife, laughing.

Mr. Hamilton laughed, too.

" And would my pretty Harriet marry him, a widower with children **?" he said.**

" Yes; it seems all **a** settled thing in her mind. She may change yet—I hope so, I am sure," Mrs. Hamilton **said,** hypocritically.

" It is not a marriage I would wish to see either; but I **will never interfere,** if you can't succeed," was Mr. Hamilton's only observation.

Mrs. Hamilton told her daughter that her father had said nothing in opposition to her marriage.

"You know, he laughs about your tall daughter : that is how he takes it. I was surprised he said so little."

"That is very well, indeed, mother."

Mrs. Hamilton's next task was to tell her sons; she told Edmund that evening; he listened very quietly.

"It is a great pity—does she do it willingly?"

"I have said all I can to her—I had other hopes for her," said his mother, with her melting voice.

"It is too bad, indeed, such a pretty girl as our Harriet; and he is so old, and has such a grown up daughter."

" But he is rich, and she will marry him, and you know there is no use in opposing her. She never speaks confidentially to me : I fear she has had some attachment—she will not tell me, but it must, from her determination, be some such motive. Do you think so, Edmund ?"

"I cannot tell : that would be sadder still."

" However, dear, let us not be unkind to her ; if she must marry him, meet him kindly —it will please her. She asked me to get you to do this. If she have sorrows of her own, we cannot wish her to speak of them now."

" No, mother, I suppose not. I shall be civil to him, you may be sure. I half fancy I know the reason of this marriage."

" He takes it better than I expected he would," thought Mrs. Hamilton. " I was afraid he would begin to remonstrate with her, and then she would have spoken about Harry and being revenged."

Mrs. Hamilton told Harriet what had passed. Harriet was still sulky—she seemed averse to any discussion—she at length brought a letter she had written to Colonel Travers to her mother : "read it, please," she said.

" It is very suitable, indeed, dear."

Harriet did not say another word; she gave short and cross answers whenever she was spoken, and would not herself speak, or in any way allude to her prospects or hopes. Her mother was very quiet and gentle, and said nothing; hoping in a day or so she would be in a more communicative mood: but Harriet sat in her room, and seemed quite pre-occupied—she ordered the pony phaeton, and drove out, but returned and still sat in her room gloomy and cross.

The next day passed, and the next, in a similar manner; she handed her mother a letter from Captain Travers.

"You see he will come for a few days next week, mother."

"Yes, and I see he talks of your being married in January ; yes, I think it is January, is it not?"

"Oh, yes; well, that is a very good time is it not, mother?"

"Oh, certainly," said Mrs. Hamilton, "but I must see about your *trousseau* immediately after Colonel Travers leaves."

"Oh, yes, so we can." And she again left without saying anything further on the subject.

The day Colonel Travers was expected, Harriet dressed herself in her prettiest and most becoming dress, and evidently took great trouble about her appearance, but was still gloomy and cross.

Colonel Travers came, a gentleman-like, formal, but very polished old man; they all received him kindly, and Harriet had nothing to complain of. His age seemed about sixty; he was pale and bald, and rather old-looking for his years; he appeared a kind and rather proud man, not extreme in any of his views, rather vain, perhaps, of just having engage d himself to one of the handsomest girls in that part of the world. He was one who fancied all women to be almost equally amiable, and that they all were quite ignorant of life in its ruder and harder outlines, whom men were to protect and guide, as he hoped to protect and guide his young bride, who would, he hoped, never know care or sorrow while he lived to guard her.

His first wife had been a woman who
realised this idea, **and in** her he fancied he
had a perfect knowledge of her sex; he wondered at the scenes he heard of in some house-
holds, and reflected with pride they were impossible in his.

Harriet received **him** with good taste,
amiably and calmly.   Her mother shone on
the occasion; she told him how " she had a
feeling of nervousness, unwillingness—what
you will—dislike, perhaps, to seeing the man
who was to **rob her** of her only daughter; but
now she had seen him, and heard him speak
—she had, indeed, **seen** him before, but it had
made no impression on her—but now she
knew him, and she **at** once felt she would
trust even Harriet to him."   She spoke with
her soft **charm,** her magic cordiality. Colonel
Travers was bewitched ; he never forgot that
winning woman, her womanly softness, her

beauty even; mild and near its setting as it was, it was not lost on him, and through all vicissitudes she kept over him the gentle influence she that day won.

Edmund, though sorry for his sister's marriage, was cordial and kind, and old Mr. Hamilton, for him, was even gay.

CHAPTER VII.

AFTER a few days stay, Colonel Travers left them.   Edmund congratulated his sister kindly as they stood in the hall, after seeing Colonel Travers off, saying how he thought him a perfect gentleman, and one with whom she could be happy, and that he, indeed, hoped she might be so.

Harriet hurried towards the stairs ; as she did so, she said—

"Thank you, Edmund, thank you ; I am sure I shall be very happy, indeed."

She spoke in a perfectly satisfied tone of voice.

Edmund thought, as she passed away— "Is she quite satisfied? Does she feel it no sacrifice? Is marriage such a great matter that for the mere point of being married people give up all hopes of realising their ideal here on earth? How is it that women persist in thinking marriage with any man a triumph and an advantage? Would not freedom be more desirable than union with one we can never love? Is solitude so painful that to escape it we must rush on all the miseries of being wedded to those with whom we can have no thought or feeling in common. Is it that—

> 'Their passions unto mine,
> Are as moonlight unto sunlight, as water unto wine?'

Can the majority of women never experience a desire or a hope, beyond the possession of diamonds, carriages, and cashmeres, as some one says? Are they willing to become the property of any man who can give them these things? I would still wish to believe there are women for whom a world were well lost. Is not Ada one? Would she not scorn such paltry lures as money, station, luxury? If she marry unhappily, it will be that she has been deceived, not that she has willingly degraded herself into a purchased toy." And then his hopes turned to the chances of undeceiving her before it was too late. "If she never marry me, I hope—I do hope, she may at least, make a happy choice, and one worthy of her."

The prayer, for it was a prayer, was unselfish; as such, we may hope it was listened to where all such are justly weighed, and find an answer in all things just.

And was Edmund right? Are there in this

world other and greater blessings than riches?
Are women wrong when they sacrifice themselves for such objects? or is the real worth
of everything the price which it will bring;
and if they can be bought, are they not, perhaps, dear enough commodities? They may
be, and probably are, many of them, incapable of any high or noble feeling; but are they
not sometimes mistaken in fancying they cannot be made to feel some of life's miseries?
Do not the purchasers sometimes care but
little for a toy when it has been played with,
and, perhaps, broken? And what of the
broken toy? I do not speak of the stronger
and bolder characters of women like Harriet,
who sacrifice themselves for ambition, or
pride, or revenge. They generally have their
reward; the world is enough for them; but
the toys, the women bought by diamonds, car-

riages, handsome dresses, what of them? The
women who never keep, for they never value
their husband's love—his purse is enough for
them.   They cease to inspire admiration
soon ; they have not dreamt such a thing was
possible ; but when it comes, are they satisfied with their fate.   I have observed them,
and found them much less satisfied than was
reasonable or just.   It is they who appear as
plaintiffs in the Divorce Court, as the interesting martyrs to fate, and they receive far more
pity than they deserve.   They are for ever
whimpering about their sufferings, and seem
to wonder men do not love them, the poor,
mean-minded, peevish things, as if they
were Beatrices and Lauras.

It had been arranged that Harriet's was
to be a gay wedding, and her friends from all
parts came to congratulate her.   She had recovered her spirits, and now seemed the

gayest of the gay; and Harry had written his congratulations and kind wishes; and Harriet read the letter with such composure, her mother hoped her dangerous dreams of revenge had passed away.

"I daresay Harry will be here," was all she said.

Mrs. Hamilton was glad, indeed; all things moved on in accordance with her wishes, and soon her anxieties would be at an end.

One day, as Edmund came in from riding, his mother told him Mrs. Alton and Ada Lowell had been paying them a visit. He was sorry he had not seen them, but Harriet said they had promised to come to the wedding; for Edmund was restless when he did not see Ada, although he seldom experienced much pleasure during the meeting.

About five days before the wedding, one

morning after Colonel Travers had left them, Harry **arrived.** He seemed anxious and excited ; he asked almost at once for Harriet. Her mother, who dreaded an interview, said that she had a headache.

" Oh, aunt," said Harry, " I must see her, I want to see her very particularly."

Mrs. Hamilton was not satisfied, but she knew it would be vain to interfere with Harriet; so she went to her room.

" Harriet," she said, as she saw her sitting writing near the fire, " Harriet, Harry has come; he is anxious to see you, he says ; some present, I suppose," added her mother, to give as conventual an air as possible to a meeting which she was afraid was not without danger.

Harriet turned paler than the paper she was writing on.

" Yes," she said.

" I could not imagine," thought Mrs.

Hamilton, "that she would be so much affected."

"I shall go, mother, and see Harry," Harriet said, but her voice was broken, her manner confused, her head bent over the paper.

"I have been writing such a number of letters," she said.

Her mother left her, feeling both disturbed and anxious. She said to Harry—

"Harriet is busy writing; she is not very well; she has been writing a great many formal letters to-day, which has knocked her up."

Harry said little, and seemed pre-occupied.

Harriet entered the room; her step was slow; she seemed going through a form, but going through it with resolution; her voice was hard and low as she said—

"You are come to congratulate me, Harry,

mamma tells me; I am very much obliged to you."

"Yes," he said, "I am come to congratulate you, and also I want a few moments conversation with you. Come into the library, uncle is gone out."

Harriet walked in; Harry went over to the window. Harriet had already seated herself at the fire.

"Harriet," he said; his voice was strange, and he did not look at her as she waited breathlessly for the next words.

"Harriet, I have got a letter in my possession."

She suddenly thrust the poker which she held deep into the fire.

"I have," he said, "a letter in my possession addressed to Miss Cavendish."

"So you are going to be married to her,

are you? You are going to be married to Miss Cavendish."

" It is not concerning my marriage with Miss Cavendish."

" What then ?" she said boldly.

" It is a letter which has been addressed to Miss Cavendish. It is anonymous, and it is full of the vilest falsehoods."

" Is it ?" she said.

" It is; and, Harriet, it is said to be in your handwriting."

" And you," she said, firmly, " you believe it ? Show me it."

He took out the letter.

" What are the vile falsehoods ?" she said.

" It says that I am a reprobate and a scoundrel, a blackguard ; there is nothing vile it does not impute to me. It warns Miss Cavendish to be on her guard, and not engage herself

to me ; and, Harriet," he concluded, " I think
it is your handwriting, and what," he said,
his passion breaking through the control in
which as yet he had kept it, " what are or
can be your motives for such low, vindictive
conduct ?"

Harriet threw her hands up before her face,
and through them he heard her words, strong
and hard—

" I loved you, and you despised me for
that girl."

" And you confess it," he said, his mind
not realising her conduct fully till she admitted it ; " you confess you acted this part
to me who had known you so long, who had
never injured you ; as to your love, it is a
mere invention. You never loved mortal."

" What," she said, starting up, " is this the
way you treat me ?—me, whom you have
driven half mad? I have loved you—I have

loved you. Give me the letter," she half screamed; "give me the letter."

"I will not," he said.

Her tone, her words hardened, and determined on getting the letter ; all concentrated on that, not the least shocked by her conduct having being exposed, or sorry for it, disgusted him.

"No," he said, "I shall certainly keep the letter."

"You intend to show it to Colonel Travers," she said, becoming suddenly quite white. She rushed towards him. "Oh! give, give me the letter."

He held it out of her reach.

"You want to ruin me, to break off my marriage. Oh ! Harry, Harry, for God's sake give me the letter. I wrote it," she said, throwing herself on her knees, "I wrote it, but I was mad. I did not know what I was doing. Oh ! Harry, give me the letter ; do not drive me out of my senses. Harry, Harry, Harry," and she clung to his arms, one of which held the letter above her. "Oh! I will do anything on earth for you if you give me it. We will all be ruined and disgraced if I am exposed. Think of my father and mother and forgive me. Oh! how —how can you be so cruel."

She moaned ; tears ran down her cheeks, and her sobs were heartrending.

"If I did give it to you," he said, " would you promise to write and say how false and cruel that letter is. Do you remember what it says? It says, owing to my conduct, my engagement with you was broken off. Do you remember the vile falsehoods about Jeanie Eames? Will you write and contradict that if I give you the letter?"

"I will, I will, I will," she said, " how can you be so cruel ?"

" You will promise to write ?"

" I was mad, I was mad. I will do anything you like."

She swayed back and forwards, as she said
these words.

" Here," he said, " here is the letter."

" Oh ! oh ! oh !" she said, as with one
bound she caught it, and in an instant it was
on the fire. She watched it blaze for a second
or two, when she started round to him.

" You fool," she said, " I don't care for you
now. I will be revenged," she screamed, " I
will. What are you to me ? Your letter,
your Miss Cavendish's letter is gone. I am
not in your power now. Begone ! I don't
care what you do. You may tell who you
like I wrote it, but I will say you are a liar
and a ruffian. Begone, sir," she said, assum-
ing the character she spoke of with a low,
sneering laugh. " I shall tell Colonel Travers

of your vile inventions, saying I had written anonymous letters. Begone out of my presence." And she laughed such a laugh as Harry never heard again. "Yesterday I was in your power, now I am not in your power, and I hate you and I despise you, you fool."

And she rushed out of the room, leaving Harry half stupefied.

CHAPER VIII.

Mrs. Hamilton came down from her room later in the day, expecting, as a matter of course, that Harry would stay for dinner. She met Harriet, who seemed in great spirits.

" Harriet," she said, " where is Harry?"

" I think he is in the stables with Edmund."

" He is gone. I saw him drive away about ten minutes after Harriet and he had that conversation in the library," said Fred.

"Is he gone? Yes, he said something about having to go, but I did not think he was serious about it."

"What did he bring you, Harriet?" said Mrs. Hamilton, expecting he had brought her some present.

"Nothing, mother; in fact, he advised me not to marry."

"Oh! so that was it," said Fred, walking off; having apparently come to the conclusion he now understood the interview perfectly, and that to listen to details was folly.

"He wished you not to marry! Why, Harriet, how strange."

"Yes, it is strange, for he did not want me to marry him; I thought men never interfered without a motive."

"Well, indeed, Harriet, it was strange; it was most uncalled for," and for once Mrs. Hamilton fully understood, as she thought, Harriet's indignation, and quite sympathised with her.

"However, mother, let it be; I can bear that, too, from Harry."

Harriet is greatly improved, her mother thought; how sensibly she now speaks about Harry.

"You have great good sense, my dear," she said, "when you take time, and are guided by it, not impulse."

"Well, I hope I may get rational by degrees. After all, the great thing is to see what can best be done; is it not?"

Mrs. Hamilton fully assented to this.

"Just so, my dear; it is very foolish to attempt impossibilities," she mechanically replied.

The wedding was to be a gay one; they were to have a long list of county families, and Harriet was to have eight bridesmaids. Ada Lowell was asked to be one; she drove over to see Harriet, to say she hoped she

would excuse her being one of the bridesmaids, as she was afraid of wearing a light
dress.

" I am not strong; I suffer from colds very
much, and my aunt would not wish me to
wear a light dress.   She thinks I might get
ill."

" I am sorry, indeed, you cannot be one,"
Harriet said, with a warmth which surprised
even herself.   " I do not wonder your aunt is
cautious; really, the dress at a wedding in
winter is ridiculous."

" You know my aunt and I are certain to
come; she is so fond of weddings."

" I always thought them stupid enough ; I
suppose I shall think the same of my own,"
said Harriet.

" Oh! one's own wedding could hardly be
stupid."   Ada blushed, fearing she spoke too
seriously.   " At least, you are so certain to

be an object of curiosity, and in your case of admiration," making her a low bow, "it will be so pleasant that you will not have left this neighbourhood altogether—that you will be within a long drive, at least."

" Have you seen my daughter-in-law? such a girl—as tall as you are. Am I not a brave woman to face such a young lady as stepmother ?"

" She seems a pleasant girl; I saw her at your ball, and I hear she is very much attached to her father."

" She may be jealous, you know," said Harriet, who had other ideas of the effect of the young lady's attachment to her father. " But come and let me show you my dresses; some of them are pretty. I have also some handsome jewellery Colonel Travers has given me."

When everything had been admired, they came down to luncheon.

Edmund was in the drawing-room. He was delighted to see Miss Lowell; was she not to be one of his sister's bridesmaids?

"I am coming to the wedding, but I am not to be a bridesmaid; my aunt fears I should get cold."

"Luncheon, Edmund dear," said Mrs. Hamilton; "take in Miss Lowell."

"I assure you, Miss Lowell, we have not seen my sister for ten minutes at a time since Colonel Travers was here last."

"Is that true?" said Ada, appealing to Harriet. "I suppose Mr. Hamilton is insinuating how vain ladies are, I think very unfairly."

"You think it is unfair for us to criticise when it all originates in a wish to attract our admiration. Is that it, Miss Lowell?"

" Did you imagine I would make a lowly supplication to be forgiven, on the plea that however mistaken our only object was to please or amuse your majesties ? If so, I think it proves that all the vanity in the world is not attached to the ladies."

" It is so pleasant to believe that one's approbation is of such immense importance to half the world, that you are very unkind, Miss Lowell, to disturb my faith in such a pleasant delusion."

" I never would have interfered with your pleasant delusion," said Miss Lowell, "if you had not been ungenerous enough to ridicule and criticise your imaginary worshippers."

" We are all fond of flattery—are we not ? And don't we generally despise the kind creatures who do flatter us ?"

" I see you at least are," said Harriet ; " the

reason, no doubt, that you accuse me of vanity, is that I have not sufficiently consulted your tastes."

" You see, Miss Lowell," said Fred, "I am considered the man of taste; my opinion is asked on all these questions. I have severally examined all my sister's dresses, and approved, with one exception—the pink moire."

" Pink suits Harriet," said Mrs. Hamilton.

" Pink," said Fred; " yes, Miss Lowell, pink suits Harriet ; but what mortal would a pink moire suit. She had a dress of crape or some gauzy stuff, looked very well; consequently, being utterly devoid of judgment, she imagines anything pink will suit her."

" What's moire ?" said Edmund, " is it satin ?"

" Satin ! no wonder my sister does not take his advice, and that he is in a huff in consequence," said Fred, with great solemnity.

"It is a rich silk, Mr. Hamilton; a watered silk."

"I think Harriet will look like a handsome housemaid, if she appears in that detestible moire; but you will see, she will never put it on. Let me choose your dress for the wedding," continued Fred.

"My dress is ordered, Mr. Hamilton; but I should like to see if there is any similarity between our tastes."

"You will wear a white bonnet; that's regulation, of course. Then, let me see—I think I should like a black lace shawl, and a grey coloured silk dress."

"Second mourning," said Harriet.

"Second mourning—you are so conventual," said Fred. "What has that to say to it."

"I think those black and white dresses

ladies have worn for the last few years look very well," Edmund said.

" Yes, I think they do. My dress is to be a pale shade of lilac—very pale, you know, with a lace shawl ; how will that look in your opinion ?"

" In my opinion, no one will look like you," said Fred.

" A very safe answer. Do you also approve, Mr. Hamilton?—after what your sister has said, I am afraid not to ask your opinion."

" What does my sister say ?"

" She says you are in a huff with her because she did not consult you about her dresses; it cannot be true—you are never in a huff.'

" Not with my sister, at all events; I have reason to be in huffs sometimes with other people, have I not?"

"I don't know about other people; but you seem to admit you are occasionally subject to huffs, do you not?"

"I am ready to confess anything."

"That sort of general confession, Mr. Hamilton, has no efficacy; you must be more particular."

"Well, then, I confess to having been in a huff the other evening."

"Without the slightest cause," Ada continued.

"No, with the very best cause," he said, looking at her.

Ada looked up; her eyes sparkled with a mischievous expression. "She knows very well how she makes me hate Bethill," thought Edmund.

"Well, be it so, Mr. Hamilton; since you say you were in a huff, I quite forgive you.

People can't be expected to have reasons for such things as huffs."

Fred, who had introduced himself into the conversation, was determined it should not be carried on without him.

" Have you lately seen Major Bethill ?" he said. "I hoped he would have committed suicide, when he heard Harriet was going to be married ; but you say he is gay and well. For my part, I despise the man."

" What is Fred saying, something about Major Bethill ?"

" Yes, just so, Harriet."

Harriet, who had little dependance on her brother's discretion, did not ask further.

" It is a long drive ; will you call for my phaeton ?" Ada said.

When Ada was bidding them good-bye,

Fred had the good nature to leave her at the drawing-room door, and let his brother see her into the phaeton. Edmund was the more delighted at this, in consequence of his uncertainty—for Fred generally did what pleased him, without much reference to other people's wishes.

As Edmund wrapped Ada up in shawls and rugs, he said—

"Have you not forgiven me? Are we not friends?"

"I wish always to remain friends," she said, as Edmund folded the fur wrapper round her in the phaeton.

Did she glance at him as he did so? His head bent down, he could not say; but as he raised his eyes, he caught her hand.

"And I," he said, "will never be willing to remain Miss Lowell's friend."

" Good-bye," was the only answer of the lady, and the little phaeton was gone.

Fred met his brother in the hall.

" You owe me those last words," he said.

Edmund laughed good-humouredly.

" Confound the fellow !" Fred thought, " he looks as if he was sure of her, and she is a deal too good for him."

CHAPTER IX.

AND Fred was not wrong; the confounded
fellow certainly looked very happy. There is
no event in our after life which has the same
effect on us, as our first hope of happiness,
where happiness is to us all important. The
fever of life is unlike any of the chronic affec-
tions; it has its crisis, when the whole mind is
engrossed by the chances of the hour, when
we breathlessly watch for the slightest symp-
tom of change, or of improvement; and with
what rapture we first recognise hope. Have

you ever watched through that period in a dear friend's life? Some of us have; we all, almost, have watched that period in the life of our love; and what is our feeling when we first recognise hope there? Is it not rapture? Doubts and fears may again over-cloud it; but how well we can remember the first hour in which we passed from anxiety to a breath-less joy. You are now perhaps changed in all respects from yourself of those days; that love may have ended in misery, you may have found happiness again; but it is not this hap-piness—or it may have been your fate to taste of first happy love; but do you forget? or is it not the most vivid and lasting memory of your life? This hour now shone on Edmund, and he, at all events, never forgot it; he rushed out of the house, he wished to be alone with his happiness. If Ada Lowell were at The Grange then, I doubt whether he would have cared to go to her. The sun had set; it was a chill, cold evening in December; he thought it lovely, that a brighter, clearer light than the light of day shone on all around. He walked fast and far, yet the whole scene was in some way photographed on his mind; he never forgot its more minute and trifling points; he could ever after recall the place at which his dog ran barking up to him, the way in which he jumped and frisked; that moon-light was unlike any other he ever saw; clouds swept over it, and it was far from full; but in his eyes, it seemed glorious and divine; he thought of it as the moon which shone in paradise of old.

And Ada Lowell, did her thoughts revert to the handsome young man who had said that he would not be willing to remain her friend? Did she hear him? and did she listen with delight, though she met it with the lying, loving, hypocrisy of women, who rely on their apparent unconsciousness as their strongest spell, to attract and to retain men's devotion. Edmund believed she did, and he thought—" I would love her less were she different from what she is." He had risen in the enthusiasm of his happiness beyond jealousy; he could, he thought, feel a friendship even for Bethill, so utterly did he ignore and despise all love, but the free, true love which Ada's unfettered fancy would bestow; and this he was now satisfied was not Bethill's.

And, Ada Lowell, what were your thoughts ? Did you not compare your two lovers? and how did the balance incline? Were the Major's practised compliments and courtesies fresh and attractive to you? Did you admire his waltzing? or did you think Hamilton better looking, with something more original about him? or did you see something

further into the character of each ? I do not
know; her face was sad, her eyes musing, her
colour did not come and go, her cheek never
brightened into smiles. Did she realise Edmund's dream? I cannot think she did. Yet
Ada told her aunt she had had a very pleasant visit at The Grange ; and they talked of
dresses for the wedding, and Ada's was to be
a pale fawn-coloured silk, with a black lace
mantle; and Ada told her aunt of Fred's ideas
about dress. And when the dress was sent
home, and Ada tried it on, her aunt said she
had never looked better. And on the morning of Harriet's wedding, as they drove over
in Mrs. Alton's brougham, she repeated the
compliment, and talked and questioned Ada
gaily as to all their doings at The Grange.
Had Mrs. Alton become Edmund's friend?
Beyond a question or two, Mrs. Alton had
never hitherto interfered with Ada's lovers ;

she seemed to have no fear of her making a
bad match, to be in no hurry that she should
make a good one. She differed from most
chaperons, she was neither anxious nor impatient.

Ada loved her aunt, she would have done
many things to please her. Whether she
would marry to please her, had never yet
become a question ; they were alike in many
points, they were both frank and sincere.
Mrs. Alton was upright, clear-sighted, and
decided. Ada, equally high-minded, was
more sensitive, and sympathetic ; there were
points in Ada's character her aunt could not
read ; there was nothing in Mrs. Alton's Ada
could not appreciate. Mrs. Alton greatly
admired Harriet that day—indeed she seemed
her husband's daughter rather than his wife.
In the old church it was a pretty scene, it
was gaily adorned, and all the gay dresses

made it look so festive and bright; but some of the party were nervous and anxious. Mrs. Hamilton fearing at the last moment she might see Harry's unwelcome face—she had become more and more sceptical about that meeting between him and Harriet. Had Harriet told her the truth? What was its meaning? or had Harriet perhaps made some mad appeal to Harry's love or pity even then? She puzzled herself over this until she was nervous and anxious. It was not until Mrs. Travers had put on her travelling dress, and the carriage was at the door, that her fears had quite subsided.

Harriet bid her mother good-bye with great composure, and Mrs. Hamilton felt how hard it was to be left with so little appearance of regret by her daughter—for she was not without some feeling; she wondered, was she to blame for her daughter's character, which she knew would come out even more strongly in her new capacity of step mother? She was more or less mystified by Harriet's marriage, which was one she could hardly feel to be flattering to her pride as a mother; but with all this mingled a sense of relief at having her daughter at length removed from her care and charge, which she had long known was but nominal, and was daily growing more intolerable to Harriet.

" I hear your nephew will soon follow Mrs. Travers' example," said old Mr. Sandford the rector of the parish, who was bidding Mrs. Hamilton good-bye.

" Oh! Have you heard he is going to be married? Do you remember the young lady's name?"

" That pretty Miss Cavendish, who was at your last ball, was the lady I heard of."

" Oh! yes; Edmund told me something of

this. Young men are in each others secrets I suppose ; but I did not think it serious ; it would be a very good thing for Harry ; I should be very glad to find it true. Good-bye."

" Did I tell you, Mrs. Alton, that people all tell me my nephew, Henry Lawson, is going to be married to Miss Cavendish; I have not yet heard it from him, but from some of Edmund's hints I fancy it's true."

" I suppose, Miss Lowell, that was the reason he would not spare us a day for our wedding."

" Edmund, you are far too discreet; I have just heard from old Mr. Sandford that Harry is to be married, and you would keep it a secret."

" Why, mother, I did not know it till this moment; it must have been Fred who has been playing some trick on poor Mr. Sandford."

" He is in great delight with your good taste and judgment in dress; has he told you so, Miss Lowell?"

" Your brother has paid me some of the prettiest compliments."

" Yes, I saw at breakfast he was beside you; I had to do the honours you know, so I could only look on from a distance."

" How I should dislike having to propose people's healths."

" You can't dislike it more than I do, it's a dreadful infliction; but I have no second sister."

" That reflection enabled you to go through this day's proceedings?"

" That, and that only."

" Did not Major Bethill make a very good speech when he proposed the bridesmaids?"

" Plenty of compliments; he must have imagined you where one of them."

" I dislike compliments extremely, one feels so ridiculous."

" You said just now Fred paid such pretty compliments."

" Yes, I believe I did; well, his compliments are so abrupt, they give one quite the idea of their being quite sincere and fresh; the Major's are too polished, and they don't seem impromptu."

" Instead of not liking compliments, you are most particular to have none but the freshest and prettiest; are not those the terms?"

"I fancy you have the same talent for them as your brother."

"I shall ask Fred to teach me a few of his; would you know them?"

" You need not pretend you don't pay compliments; were you not paying Miss Blackall some the other evening?"

" Yes I was; I said I knew she would look well in a riding hat."

" That is not a compliment; that's quite true she would look very well."

" And are all compliments untrue? or will a thing being true prevent its being a compliment?"

" I think it will; I think a compliment is always an exaggeration."

" Then if I were to say you look far better than Miss Blackall in a hat, that would be, I suppose, no compliment?"

" You never saw her in one, so you cannot judge; therefore it is a compliment, and it is neither fresh nor pretty. You must, I am afraid, get Fred to teach you some of his."

" Ada, dear, the brougham has come; good-bye. Mr. Hamilton, I had a very good view of your riding the last day at Sefton; I saw you for half-a-mile, and was delighted at the way you took the stream. Come, Ada, have you on your shawl ?"

" Yes, thank you, Mr. Hamilton; it's in the carriage. Good-bye."

Although Major Bethill paid Ada very little attention on this occasion, he had been making inquiries about her, and he had come to the conclusion he could do nothing better than marry her; he calculated the amount of her fortune as sure to be something handsome if her aunt approved, and he admitted it would be better for him to marry soon, as if he delayed much longer it might be difficult to do so with the same advantage; he wound up by saying he knew how a lady should be treated, and in him Miss Lowell would be sure of a good husband. And he meant it to a certain extent; he did not intend to spend her money, or desert her, or ill-treat her; he intended, as he said, to make Ada a good

husband, and he had little **doubt of** her ac-
quiesence. He had received **a great** deal of
civility from her aunt, **which** was meant **for**
encouragement he was convinced; and Ada,
too, had been at all times agreeable and pleasing. There **had been a period** when he was
much perplexed what **to** decide on, fearing
Ada might accept him, **although** her aunt
might not approve; **in** this case what a posi-
tion he would be in—obliged to take the lady
and **lose the** money. But of late he had taken
courage, hoping Mrs. Alton was not too
averse, or the young **lady** too **much** inclined
for the match; but what more **than** all else
decided him was a rumour that his regiment
might be sent abroad that spring. It had not
been thought likely that they would have left
England for another year; but some disturb-
ance in Canada had given rise to a report that
they might be ordered out **this** spring; if so

haste was indispensable, for heiresses in Canada were few, he remembered. Mrs, Alton had that morning at the wedding breakfast given him an invitation to dinner for some day the following week, and he determined to know his fate then.

CHAPTER X.

ADA and her aunt were busily engaged gar-
dening; Mrs. Alton was very fond of flowers.
There was a pretty grass garden under the
drawing-room windows, where there was
always a choice collection of flowers; it was
well sheltered and laid out with taste, and
from it the shrubberies extended for some
distance. Ada also was fond of flowers, and
willingly assisted her aunt in all her garden-
ing operations. They were having the pleasure ground tidied and brushed up to-day, the

early snowdrops were out in numbers, and
the February air had quite a spring feel. Ada
heard a horse's foot passing towards the hall
door. Mrs. Alton told the gardener to see
who it was; but before he had reached the
door Major Bethill had come forward towards
them, followed by the gardener. Mrs. Alton
was glad to see him, he was rather a favourite
of hers; from him she was sure to hear of all
the news going, for he soon identified himself
with whatever place he was in, and made
himself aware of all its goings on. He was
always exceedingly attentive to Mrs. Alton;
indeed, he talked far more to her than to her
niece, which perhaps contributed to his
popularity with her. Mrs. Alton was anxious
to know how it was he had not been able to
dine with them about a week before.

"You mentioned you had to leave on

military duties; is there any truth in the report of your being moved, I have heard something of it?"

"I should not be at all surprised if we were. There is some report going, but nothing special as yet; some people think we will be sent to Portsmouth, and then on to India."

"You may meet my father then," said Ada; "you know he has been in India five-and-twenty years, Major Bethill."

"I have heard, I think, that he is in the Punjaub."

"Yes," Mrs. Alton said; "he is very fortunate, he is in a good climate, and likes it very well."

"I fear, if we should be sent to India, it will be to Madras; there are regiments coming home from Madras, and none this year from the northern provinces."

" Madras is not nearly as good a climate; it is very hot indeed, I believe."

" I should like to see India; but I should not like to pay it a long visit," said Ada.

" It is a bad place for ladies," said Major Bethill, thinking of the chances of Mrs. Alton not approving of the match.

" Oh! Major Bethill, I was under the impression all ladies liked India; they are so flattered and in such request out there."

" But, Miss Lowell, the heat, the fevers, the mosquitoes," said Bethill, gloomily. " I should be sorry to trust my wife out there, if I had a wife."

" You will be sure to marry in India if you go," said Mrs. Alton, laughing. " I shall watch the *Times*, I am sure I shall see you gazetted soon after you go out. It is always so, my brother met both his wives in India.

Why I suppose young Hamilton won't be there a year until he is married."

"Ah! young fellows like Hamilton do those things, though how a subaltern can marry I for one never could understand. We have not had a day's hunting lately, Miss Lowell."

"No; nothing at all near us."

Mrs. Alton was called into the house; Major Bethill walked round the grass garden with Ada, admiring any of the spring flowers which had already peeped over ground.

"This is really a very pretty spot," he said, "and the walks are so well laid out; you have a great deal of fine shrubbery."

They walked on a little to a point from which the old house looked well.

"Had I a place like this I am sure I should feel sorry to leave it."

"Yes; I think it is pretty, and I should certainly feel sorry to leave poor old Sefton."

"You probably will not leave it for any length of time."

"I suppose I never shall; my aunt objects to my even going to see my father, though I should only stay a year or so, and I should greatly like it."

"She is quite right, India is not for such as you; that may do for young ladies who go there to seek their fortunes, but you need not go there to seek yours."

Ada laughed. "I am glad of that, I should not like to go to India to seek my fortune, as you say."

"Oh, no! young ladies generally go there who find it hard to get husbands at home, but that never could be your case," the Major said, rather familiarly.

" Oh! we may suppose that all ladies do not go with that object."

"'Pon my word, they very generally do. I can't agree with you there, Miss Lowell, but as I said, Miss Lowell is not one of those young ladies.

" No," Bethill said—at last dashing into the subject, and with all his experience awkwardly enough; but it is so difficult to approach such a matter-of-fact listener as Ada with any enthusiasm, even if the Major's strong point had been enthusiasm. " No," he said; " but, Miss Lowell, might I venture to ask, to hope you would make such a sacrifice for me—could I hope you would leave England with me ?"

Ada listened to this sudden, and to her unexpected speech, with half doubt as to its meaning.

" With you ?" she said slowly.

" Yes; with me," the Major said, "as my wife —could I but hope you would care for me sufficiently to do so, I would indeed be perfectly happy. I know," he said, for Ada had made no answer, "how bad a match I am in the eyes of the world, but, dear Miss Lowell, I have never seen any one whom I cared for before, and this must excuse me, this will, I know, excuse me," he continued, as he put out his hand to take hers.

Miss Lowell drew back in the smallest possible degree from Major Bethill's side, " you are really—you are serious in this," she said, as if half doubting still.

The Major was beginning to again protest his sincerity, but she gently stopped him.

" I am so ashamed that I should not have foreseen this—I am really—indeed, sorry," she added, her beautiful face softening as she spoke, and kindling into blushes, " but I never—"

Bethill interrupted her; " do not say you do not love me," he said, at last awake to the bearing of her words.

" Believe me, I regret all this, I do indeed, you will forgive me, when I tell you I never once imagined you were serious."

" Have I not at all times shown you how much I admired you; how could you doubt it ?" he asked.

" I did not think it more than a mere passing admiration; you will forgive me, it can never be;" she spoke slowly, and her face was bent on the ground.

" Do not refuse me some hope, you love no other; why then may I not hope at some future day."

" It can never be," Ada said slowly.

" Why ?" said Bethill, getting heated and

angry, "is it because you love some other, because you love young Hamilton?"

"You have no reason whatever for supposing so," she said, her voice sinking lower and lower, "and it is unkind to us both."

"Do you mean to deny he loves you," said the Major, with a scornful laugh.

"I have not the slightest reason for supposing he does," she said, influenced by the rudeness of Bethill to tell a particularly innocent untruth.

"Then pardon me," he said, "you are indeed very dull."

Ada had made every allowance for his manner up to this point, for she was too generously minded not to regret the position in which, as she thought, her own blunder had placed him; but it was now becoming so extremely unpleasant to her, she at length said—

"All this, Major Bethill, has really nothing whatsoever to say to the matter."

"Excuse me," he said, "for thinking it has a great deal to say to the matter," and bowing to Ada, he walked towards the house without any further farewell.

"I really am sorry," Ada thought, "though the Major is evidently an ill-tempered man, and takes my refusal very badly; still I am sorry aunt liked him; it was pleasant to her to see him, and now I have evidently made an enemy of him, and he is very cross and touchy. How at once he began about poor Hamilton; I wonder would he act in the same way, but I am to blame myself, greatly to blame;" for Ada generally blamed herself when anything unpleasant occurred.

In the meantime the Major had returned to the house, and as he approached he saw Mrs.

Alton on the steps; " Dear Mrs. Alton, I want to speak a few words to you," he said.

Mrs. Alton walked into the drawing-room.

"I have," Major Bethill began, "been speaking to your niece, Mrs. Alton; I have, in fact," he said, with an appearance of frankness very well assumed, "I have, in fact, been asking her to marry me."

"Can she have accepted him; why else should he tell me," flashed through Mrs. Alton's mind, as she looked up in great surprise. " Yes," she said, as she sat down on one of the sofas near the window.

Major Bethill saw the expression of her face. " It is," he said, " unusual for a gentleman to speak of these matters, except the young lady receives them favourably; but in this case there is so much that is perplexing; so much in fact which I cannot understand, that I address myself to you, dear Mrs.

Alton " Mrs. Alton was too good a diplo-
matist to do more than smile and bow. "Miss
Lowell has at all times been so flattering in
her manner, has received me so favourably,
that," he said, " her conduct to-day has been
doubly painful to me; she seems incapable of
coming to any decision," he added gently.

"She has been, perhaps, surprised," said
Mrs. Alton; "you can at once see Ada is
nothing of a coquette, Probably, Major Bethill,
she never calculated on a very probable
result," said her aunt, smiling.

"I am sure—indeed, I know," continued
Bethill, " she would never do anything you
would disapprove of: she loves you more than
a mother, and, indeed, deservedly," said he,
warmly. "And I, I do assure you, would
not wish her to act in opposition to your
wishes. No—when I know your wishes on
the subject," said the Major, magnanimously,

" if you tell me you disapprove of my addressing your niece, it will be quite enough for me. I know it would not in the world's eyes be a good match—the world will say I am old enough to be her father, and not in any way good enough for her : and you, Mrs. Alton, may justly think so too."

" I hope Ada has not been telling him the whole objections are on my part," thought Mrs. Alton ; " it is not her style, she generally has courage enough to say what she thinks—but then, indeed," she indulgently concluded, " she may hardly have known what to say to this Major Bethill, for I hardly know myself."

" I assure you, Major Bethill, upon my part, I am perhaps peculiar; but I do not like interfering in these matter, I leave it all to the young ladies. If Ada has made up her mind to marry you—"

The Major eagerly interrupted.

" Not at all, nothing of the kind—do not for a moment think so—but your wishes, your views, I know, have greater influence over her than you imagine—than you desire, perhaps," he added, seeing Mrs. Alton **was** about to **speak.** " But, **as** I said before, my dear Mrs. Alton, in everything I am ready to be guided **by** your wishes, if, as you say, your opinions are opposed to taking any steps,—whatever your **views are, I** will act in strict obedience to them."

" You are very good, indeed," she said ; " nothing can be more handsome. I assure you, I never have "—she changed the word— " I never do interfere with Ada. I have per- fect trust in her; she, I hope, knows I will never oppose anything which is for her hap- piness. Can I say more, Major Bethill?" she added, kindly.

"My dear friend, you cannot indeed. I make but one more request: will you yourself tell Ada this? it will remove all misconceptions from her mind. But might I venture to hope I have your good wishes?" he said, rising to leave.

"I can only repeat," Mrs. Alton said, "I have not the slightest objection; but with Ada, Ada herself, the whole matter lies."

"One thing more," he said, turning round, "might I hope you would do one thing for me—would you let me know the result after you have spoken to your niece?"

"I will—certainly; and I hope in any case we shall always remain good friends."

"You need not make that request," he said, gallantly. "Good-bye, Mrs. Alton, good-bye."

After the Major had left, Mrs. Alton sat musingly at the fire.

"I do not think she in the least cares for

him," she thought, " and why he made such a fuss—asking me to write and all that—I cannot understand. She is very pretty, very attractive—I suppose she will take a fancy to some one some of these days—in the meantime I do not wonder at many being attracted by her. I am glad, though, it is not Major Bethill : I do not think he cares for her—he is not the person for her, at all events. I suppose she will tell me—at least I must speak to her before I write to Major Bethill. I imagine Hamilton fancies her, too," and Mrs. Alton smiled.

Ada came in shortly.

" Ada," said her aunt, " Major Bethill has been talking to me, and of you, too."

" Oh! has he aunt—what did he say ?"

" He said he had asked you to be his wife, and he said he hoped I would speak to you, and say I had no objection."

" And, aunt, what did you say to him ?"

" I said, my dear, I would speak to you, and say I had no objection."

"You know, aunt dear, I would never marry him; you know that," Ada said, with tears in her eyes.

" Yes, Ada, I felt sure of that; but I spoke to him civilly, of course—he deserves that at least—but I did not expect that you would have him."

" I would not wish to be unkind; indeed, I think it was all caused by my own stupid blindness: I should have seen it, I know, aunt."

" That would have been no use with Major Bethill: he asked me to write and tell him your ultimate decision when you had spoken to me, or I to you rather, and told you I did not object."

Ada laughed. " Did he really, aunt? he

could not have had any doubt about my decision, I should have thought; indeed, he told
me he supposed I fancied some one else."

" How did it all happen ?"

" We were walking together, talking of
India; he asked me would I go there as his
wife.   I said, ' No ;' he seemed very much
surprised, and suggested I liked some one else.
I got a little angry, and said I did not," and
Ada coloured deeply.

" You did well, dear: he never would have
suited you."

" He never would, indeed, aunt ; and really
I never once thought of such a thing as his
proposing for me ; but I am sure he is very
angry, he will never forgive me—he is one
never would I should think.   Oh, dear ! it
is very unfortunate every way."

"Now, Ada, about the letter—that is the
next point—I think you should write it."

" No, indeed, aunt; you agreed to that."

" Well, I need not write until to-morrow; but the Major will tell everybody that only for me you would have married him, and show my letter very likely as a proof of it."

" He never would do that."

" Oh! child, you do not know these people as well as I do."

" But why need he talk of it at all?"

" Nothing will persuade him that you and I won't talk of it, and he will wish to tell his own story first."

" If you were good-natured, aunt, you would take him yourself!"

" Come, Ada, how shall we begin the letter ?—' Dear Major Bethill, I find you misunderstood my niece:' that would never do—that he would say showed I had forced you to change your mind, and he would show my letter about."

"Oh! aunt, what a horrid bore it is! Could you not see him?"

"I could not, dear; if I asked him here without answering, or, I mean, writing to tell him of your ideas being different from what he imagined them to be, he would say I had treated him very badly."

"It is too bad altogether, for I know he will be so angry and spiteful."

"Well, dear, all the better for you, you are not to be his wife."

CHAPTER XI.

" WHAT do you say to this letter, Ada; I wrote it last night:—

" DEAR MAJOR BETHILL,—

" I fulfilled my promise, but do not find my doing so has altered my niece's ideas, as you hoped it might have done. She joins me in hoping you will always believe how sincerely I wish to

" Remain, yours affectionately,

" EDITH ALTON.

" Sefton Hall, Friday evening."

" Is it not very short, aunt ?"

" You see, dear ! what is there to say ? I wish it to be such a letter as cannot be shown, and one which, if left about, will not in any way commit you—under these circumstances it is difficult to be fluent."

" Yes, aunt, I suppose it will do very well; but it does seem very short and stiff."

So the letter lay on the table, but in the evening, with some slight modification, it was sent.

The following day Major Bethill was some-what anxiously expecting this letter; when he spoke to Mrs. Alton, he did so to present matters in a different light to her, without much expectation of any satisfactory result; but in the two days which had since elapsed he had cheated himself into imagining it was by no means improbable that Mrs. Alton's in-fluence, which he was sure he had secured might overcome Ada's reluctance. It was not love that led him into this delusion, I need hardly say; Ada was merely the representative in his eyes of at the least thirty thousand pounds, perhaps ultimately far more: this was a sum which he greatly wished to have transferred to his bankers, and Ada followed it as a necessary incumbrance. Not that Major Bethill particularly disliked Ada, or preferred any one else. His views were that he wanted money, and must marry for it—to the lady he was quite indifferent. He had reason to fear the rumour was correct, and that his regiment would be sent abroad in spring : he expected the Colonel would soon sell, and he had no money to purchase, and in India or Canada— for there were some who thought they would be sent to Canada—it was much more difficult to find ladies with money than at home.

On the following morning, when his old soldier servant came in with his **water for** shaving, and brought his letters, he at once guessed Mrs. Alton's, and seized and tore it open. It was so short; he had read it in an instant, when the first thing he did was to throw one of **his** shoes after the old servant as he went to the door.

"Stop," he said, "you cursed fool, do you call this hot water? Bring me some more hot water at once; **do you** hear? hot water, **you fool**."

"Yes, sir," said the old fellow, not a muscle of his face moving, but retreating rapidly towards the **door; but** when he had shut it, rubbing his leg, **he** muttered—"What the devil ails the Major; I never saw him worse since he lost so much on the Derby."

Bethill walked up and down his room in a **perfect fury.**

"Confound her," he said, "it is just what I might expect. What am I to do now? And the regiment nearly sure to go abroad, How am I to get any one else now? It's that d——d Hamilton she is running after—like Kate Lawton, I lost all my time with at Leamington, and then her ass of a brother is the first to tell me she is to be married to Sir John Dalton, after throwing me over; but they are all alike, a scheming, cheating lot, ready to sell you any moment they get a chance. What a set I have had to deal with —that one, and the Manchester girl, and this Ada Lowell, tossing up her head after keeping one a whole year dancing with her. Devil take her," said the Major, with a heartiness that could not be questioned.

"What will I do now? Where shall I get the money for the step? And it is sure to go

in the regiment soon. Confound it; and
there is no one I know now would have me
on a sudden since Ellen Broughton is married. I was always sure of five thousand
there, for I could have had her at any time;
It is the devil's thing altogether."

And the Major walked up and down, mut-
tering and cursing.

The old servant came in again with the
water; the Major growled and took it. As he
shaved, he still growled and cursed at intervals.

" I am growing an old man ; I suppose it
is all up with me now.   I suppose I will have
to end by marrying Ellen's sister Jane. My
sister was always talking to me of Ellen, but
I think she had some idea I fancied her, and
she was the best looking.   Confound them
all, they are the deuce's lot ; but a girl like
Jane ought to snap at a Major in the army ;

she has not more than five thousand. I wonder has she got it though."

He took up the letter again.

"Her niece joins her," he said "if there is a hypocritical cheat alive, it is that very niece of yours. Confound you, and her ; I will give some of the fellows, Cole and one or two of them, an idea how the case really is, for that pair will have a fine story about me in a day or two: but I will take a march on them there," said the Major with a grin.

"I wonder where Cole is," said Bethill, shortly afterwards, as he walked out of the mess-room. " Did you see him, Lloyd ?"

" Yes, I saw him crossing the barrack yard just now ; I suppose he is at the ratting match with the young fellows."

"It is very likely ; it is just the folly he delights in," muttered Bethill, who soon after met Cole. " He is the person to speak to ;

his wife will spread it far and near," thought
Bethill.

" What is doing to-day, Cole ?"

" Not much ; some of them talk of going
out coursing, and Galton is busy with the new
ensign killing rats with his terriers."

" Did you hear the latest news ?   Gad ! sir,
I have got the sack at Sefton."

Cole looked up with a half-surprised, half-
knowing air.

"It is the best thing going, sir ; regular
remonstrance ; has other views for her niece ;
don't come again ; all the rest of it."

" You don't say so," said Cole.

" Yes, 'pon my life, when I went there last,
the old lady and I had a long confab ; she
hoped I would not persist in coming, should
send her niece away, and so on."

"What an old cat ; did you see the
girl ?"

"Hunted, sir ; hunted, by Jove! Gad! the girl wàs nothing to me but a nice girl; but the old cat took alarm."

"What a confounded shame," said Cole.

"The worst of it is, I have to go down to my people immediately; just got a letter from them to-day, so I will not be able to torment the old lady for the next fortnight, at all events."

"I am going to the orderly room. Come on, Bethill."

" My dear fellow I can't; I must see that blackguard servant of mine packs my clothes; he is a horrid rascal."

" What is he up to now," said Cole ; " is he trying to humbug me? What's the row been about at Sefton ?"

Major Bethill lost no time in getting his fortnight's leave, and was gone that very day, intending to have it extended, and hoping the regiment would be at Portsmouth before he returned.

Captain Cole at once went home to tell the great intelligence to Mrs. Cole.

"There has been a pretty row between Bethill and the people at Sefton," said he.

"Has there?" said Mrs. Cole; "how did you hear it? What was it about? Was it about the heiress?"

"Just so. I don't know what it was; but **Bethill came up to** me in the barrack yard as I was going to the orderly room."

"Yes," said his wife, impatiently.

"**And** he rushes at me at once, just as I was saying that Galton and the new ensign were having a match with their terriers."

"Yes, yes."

"And he begins—'Cole, did you hear I got the sack at Sefton.' Why, I never heard such a queer thing before. And just as I was saying, 'Come on, Bethill, to the orderly room,' expecting to hear something about it all, he says, 'I must see that rascal of mine packs my clothes ;' and off he bolts."

"And he told you nothing but that?"

"He told me nothing but that he had got the sack from the old lady ; not come again ; other views for her niece; so on."

"Did he tell you that ?"

"Yes, he did, of course ; that was what he did tell, you know."

"She has refused him," said Mrs. Cole, with the decision of a field marshal; "if you don't see it, I do."

"Gad! that is just what I thought ; I thought you'd say that," said Cole ; "I said, coming across, you would, two to one."

"Tell me exactly what he said," said the lady, who now listened to all the windings of

Cole's story with the greatest interest, and
when he had concluded, repeated her opinion,
" It is nothing, but that she has refused him.
What do you think, Tom ?"

" I thought he was trying to humbug me
the moment he left me."

" I wonder he did not succeed," said Mrs.
Cole ; " you know, Tom, it has been done."

Tom laughed, for he was a good-humoured
fellow, and sauntered off to tell his tale to the
others, as he said ; and before Bethill had
taken his ticket, his whole affairs were dis-
cussed by his friends—how he had played his
cards, why he lost, and finally why he now
ran off.   It was decided that he was nothing
but a fool, to think that a girl with so much
money would have him, the general idea
being her aunt wanted a sprig of nobility for
her, nothing less, as Bethill himself had
said.

CHAPTER XII.

"WELL, Ada; I have been cross-questioned about you and Major Bethill to-day, so you see that was not long a secret," said Mrs. Alton, as she came into the drawing-room where Ada was sitting.

"Who spoke to you about it, aunt?"

"Old Mr. Sandford—you know he hears all the news going." Mrs. Alton was herself fond of gossip, still she never failed to comment on Mr. Sandford's failing, though she largely availed herself of it.

"What did he say about it, aunt?"

"He said, 'I think Mrs. Alton you were quite right, not to countenance Major Bethill's paying your niece such particular attention.' And I said, 'That is all over, Mr. Sandford; 'Yes,' he said, 'you were quite right, it was a very wise precaution.' 'What precaution?' said I; he then told me he heard that I had requested Major Bethill not to come here. I said I never did such a thing, that you were able to take care of yourself, and then in fact I told him the whole story."

"Oh, aunt; I am sorry you said anything about it."

"Not at all dear, when people are talking, it is just as well to tell what has really happened; but did I not guess what Major Bethill would do? they say the whole regiment are off before he returns."

"Why, where is he?" said Ada.

" Gone to his sister's, who lives near Bath, I believe; gone for the last fortnight. I met the two Hamiltons, and Fred has passed his examination, but does not know what regiment he will get into; he said leaving, he and his brother would ride over to bid us good-bye before he left; do you know I like Fred Hamilton," said Mrs. Alton, as she went away to take off her bonnet.

A day or two after, Ada and her aunt were sitting at breakfast in a small room in the front of the house, which Mrs. Alton liked to sit in in the morning; it was an ante-room through which you passed into the drawing-room, but it had a southern aspect which the drawing-room had not.

" Here is a letter from Charlie!"

Mrs. Alton took up the letter eagerly, it had a foreign post mark, " somewhere from South America," she said, looking at the letter; as some people have a habit of doing before reading it.

"Where is he now, aunt?"

Mrs. Alton opened the letter. "At Valparaiso, he says he will see us very soon, that they were nearly wrecked lately, but he supposes we know more about that than he, by this time, some fighting between the small kingdoms out there; he says. I really don't know what he means; he hopes he will see us all in early spring. I suppose this is early spring, although it does not look very like it to-day." It was snowing, with a bitter wind, a real March day.

"Why, he will be here immediately, aunt; that will be very pleasant."

"Yes, I am very fond of Charlie; I daresay he is a very fine young man now, he is three-and-twenty, I believe; how strange it seems to me. I remember your father and his mother little things, when I was married, and they are both gone, I may say, for I shall never see your father, Ada."

" Indeed you will, aunt; and all my host of brothers and sisters, they will be home before long, I daresay."

" I don't think, dear, I would care to see them so much, I was very fond of your mother, and it seems odd to me his being married again—but men are different from us, they don't remember long—I believe his present wife is very handsome."

Ada said nothing.

It is not in woman, be she ever so angelic, to forgive her father for a second marriage.

" Indeed that photograph shows she is."

" Yes," said Ada, " I have always heard she is very handsome, she is fair. Am I like my mother?" she asked.

" No, dear; you are far more like your

father, I am very fond of your father, though
I have been disappointed about his marrying,
when after all it was the best thing he could
do; but somehow one sometimes would as
soon people did not do the best thing for
themselves."

"Aunt, is Charlie like my Aunt Ada?"

"Very, yes very; his father was a sad sort
of man, I wondered how she fancied him, but
he was ill, that was the reason he was so low
spirited I suppose, consumptive—all the
Domvilles were."

"Charlie is not much of a Domville then,
aunt."

Mrs. Alton laughed, "Not much; I think
we will have him here very soon." She then
went off to see after her housekeeping, leaving
Ada sitting drowsily at the fire, seeing
pictures in it, perhaps.

So great was her absorption, that though

not nervous she started at a fierce knock at the hall door, given by cold, impatient fingers, and the moment after the two Hamiltons were ushered in; for Mrs. Alton was at home to every one, if she was anywhere about the place.

"How do you do, won't you come near the fire, what a day?" said Ada.

"Dreadful," said Fred, "but my days are limited, you know."

"How are you, Mr. Hamilton, did you venture out?" said Ada.

"Yes, was it not very heroic of me?"

"He has been complaining of the weather bitterly since he came from Paris," said Fred.

"Paris, were you away?" Ada said.

"I was in Paris, doing best man for Harry Lawson, I was there nearly three weeks."

"I never saw his marriage."

"You will to-night, I hope; I forgot putting

it into the papers, and I suppose I should have done so, as no one else has."

" Miss Cavendish is the lady, is she not?"

" Oh, yes; we had a very gay wedding— they are gone to Rome, and are not to return for a long time; I fancy she likes foreign life better than England."

" And you are going to join your regiment so very soon, Mr. Hamilton?"

"In a month I am to join the 159th, they are in Malta."

" Oh, how are you, you have had such a day," said Mrs. Alton, who had just entered the room ; " are you frozen?"

" I rather like such a day as this, I quite prize it, in anticipation of my summer in Malta," said Fred.

"I have had a letter from my nephew, Charlie Domville, saying he will be over with us immediately ; he is in the navy you know, and has been in South America for a long time ; do you remember him at all ?"

" I do not, Mrs. Alton, very indistinctly at least, I think I must have been at school when he was here last. Have you heard we have lost Major Bethill ?"

" I heard he had gone to Bath."

" Yes, he will be Colonel in a few days, Colonel Stewart has sold, and Major Bethill is to get the step, we went to pay Bethill a visit yesterday, but found he had gone ; they say he is engaged to a girl with a good deal of money."

" Engaged !" said Mrs. Alton, with the slightest possible surprise in her tone of voice.

" Yes," said Fred, " to a doctor's daughter, a Miss Broughton or Bolton, I forget which, Captain Cole told us ; I think he said he had had a letter from the Major, he said it had been a long time going on."

"Oh! has it?" said Mrs. Alton.

"Yes, so Cole said; but Mrs. Cole says he is quite wrong, that it was a sister of this girl's that he used to pay attention to. However, she told us," said Fred, laughing, "she had written to a friend in Bath, to hear the particulars."

"And it is a very good match," said Mrs. Alton, "I am glad of that, Major Bethill you know would like a little money."

"Oh, a very good match I believe, her elder sister is married to a Colonel Johnstone. I suppose he will be married before they sail."

"Have you seen your sister lately?"

"I am going over there next week, and they are to return with me, for a few days, they are not long at home; we have had two weddings very near each other, hers and Harry's."

" Very, indeed. Your brother was in Paris, was he not? You had a gay wedding in Paris, had you not, Mr. Hamilton?"

"Oh! very. The French people admired Miss Cavendish so much, too, it was amusing."

" I thought her very pretty, and graceful, and so fair," said Mrs. Alton.

" Yes, everyone thinks so; I don't admire that description of beauty so much myself; she looks so white and inanimate; she is a golden-haired blonde though, and that is the rage just now, I believe."

" The Empress of the French style," said Ada.

" But the Empress of the French has such a pensive, soft expression of face; she is not white and inanimate."

" The fact is," said Fred, " Edmund likes

a bit of a Tartar; he has often confessed his partiality for strong-minded ladies."

" Anything before a very amiable one, Mr. Hamilton. A young lady with a high reputation for amiability is very hazardous; they are, indeed; be warned in time," said Mrs. Alton.

" Oh! you need not warn him—it's quite the other way. You will hear of him being beaten by his wife, and consoling himself, like Lord Derby's Irishman, that it amuses her, and does not hurt him."

" And would it not be very consoling ?" said Edmund. " What do you think, Miss Lowell ?"

" I have no doubt if you fancied a lady of that character you would console yourself in some such way."

" You have paid me a great compliment by

the observation; you give me credit for being able to read the lady's true character, and being anything but fickle; high praise, certainly."

" I think if people like each other, they generally do read character pretty accurately, that there is not as much delusion as one hears of in books."

" Because books, generally," said Edmund, "speak of a very second-rate sort of love; fancy, admiration, without any sincere sympathy, or high feeling !"

" Why, I did not think you were such a critic.   Are you a great novel reader ?" said Ada.

" I read a great many, but then I am seldom satisfied; perhaps the love I am thinking of is more fit for poetry."

" Well, I hope the strong-minded lady will

be poetical, if she is as fierce as you seem to expect."

"I won't so much mind her being fierce, if she will only love me, as I long to be loved; but I should never be satisfied if she did not," Edmund said, speaking very fast and low.

"Mr. Hamilton," said Ada, in her usual tone of voice, "did I tell you that we are expecting my cousin Charlie Domville home immediately?"

"Are you?" said he; "I knew him tolerably well when he was last here; I am sure he must be delighted to return home," said Edmund, looking at Ada, "I should, if I were he."

"Oh! of course he is delighted; I heard aunt asking your brother to come over and see him when he arrives."

"You will, I hope, Mr. Hamilton; there

must be shooting, or fishing, or some sort of amusement going on; and you would oblige me so, you and your brother, by coming over, and seeing if you can in any way amuse yourselves."

"I shall be delighted, Mrs. Alton."

"I suppose Charlie is not much of a sportsman?" said Ada.

"I think he is," Edmund said, "but I almost forget; I remember him very well though; he was very good-looking and pleasant; but I forget about the sport."

"Yes, he is so good-natured; I like sailors so much."

"They say all ladies do; they are greater, favourites than the military heroes," said Edmund, "are they not?"

"Oh! yes; far greater. I don't like military men—that is, I mean," she said, "the more military they are in manner, the less I like them."

"We went to pay Major Bethill a visit; he was away; but we heard he was going to be married."

Ada blushed, thinking he meant to refer to his marriage with her.

"Oh! is he?" she said, awkwardly.

"Yes, to a Bath lady, a Miss Broughton. Cole said he had written to say he would purchase the Colonelcy, as he was to be married to a lady with some money; and her friends advised his doing so, so Cole said; he won't re-join the regiment here, I believe."

"I am very glad to hear he is going to make such a good match; he is a pleasant little man."

"I hope, Mr. Hamilton, we will soon have the hounds in the neighbourhood," Mrs. Alton said, when they were at lunch.

" I think it is very probable we shall after this frost; if they come, will you, Miss Lowell, let me take care of you? I shall then believe you have forgiven me," he said, in a lower voice.

" I don't know, Mr. Hamilton; in the first place, probably my cousin will be at home; then I shall have him, of course, as an escort; it would be rude not, you know."

" What is the second place, for I cannot but hope he won't be home?"

" I cannot forget about the last hunt; you will perhaps quarrel with me again."

" I could not quarrel now," Edmund said.

" Come, Edmund, we must start soon."

" Indeed, I believe we should, it's getting a fine evening, too. How well the garden looks from this point, and the cover-side." He walked towards the window, beside which

K 2

Ada was standing. "So you won't promise me the pleasure of taking care of you, even for one day, Miss Lowell? Do not refuse me," he said, in the softest tone of a very soft voice.

"It is better I should, Mr. Hamilton, far better;" and she, too, spoke low as a whisper.

"For once even, only once."

"Even for once, it is better not."

Her eyes were bent on the floor determinately; she must have heard the horse's feet on the gravel, and Fred bidding her aunt goodbye; but she never lifted them in the slightest degree. She put out her hand in a timid, frightened way, as if afraid it would be repulsed; but her eyes were never raised. Edmund thought he understood her; he caught the small hand gently.

"Good-bye," he said, "Miss Lowell." He had bid her aunt good-bye; and, almost as she thought in an instant, was gone.

CHAPTER XIII.

"He loves me; yes, he loves me," Ada said again and again, as she sat brooding over the fire, after the brothers had gone; "and I—I never loved, I cannot love anyone, it seems to me; I have no wish to be anyone's wife, I am happy as I am; I care for him enough to be sorry he loves me, that is all; but I should not let him love me, I should in no way encourage it. Why should he, too, have it in his power to reproach me? Did not Major Bethill say, I must be very dull if I did not see it ? Did he not laugh at my denying Hamilton loved me ? sneering at me as a coquette, and would he not be right, would I not be a coquette? Yes," she said, " I am sorry to say it ; I despise myself for it ; but I would wish him to go on loving me, though I would never love him, though I could not marry him. I would be mean and cowardly ; I would let him love me, rather than give myself pain by telling truth." And she hung her head, and the large tears rolled from her eyes. She cried like a child for her lost lover, and the bitter sense of shame mingled with her tears. She had ceased to be a child ; she had ceased to find doing what was right, brought constant, unfailing pleasure, as of old. She had struggled, she had done right, and she thought she would do it again ; but she felt sad, not content. " Was Edmund now sure to hate her because she would not marry him?" she asked herself. "Was it possible ? Could she ever have married him?" And her whole nature seemed to recoil from the very idea. "I will never marry, I feel I never could," she said. "No, I was right, I could not marry him; and to let him go on loving me, after I knew it, and knew my own feelings, that was impossible. I would have been, I ought at least to have been, more unhappy, acting so unfeelingly." And again her tears came heavy and fast. "There is one thing only I can do for him now," she said, "conceal that he loved me; he will thank me for that when he has forgotten this fancy. I would wish him to be my friend, but he never will; he hates me at this moment. I liked him, and we might have been friends; but I could not marry him."

Poor Ada, she would have wished to have

talked with her aunt about this, but she thought it would not be fair to Hamilton.

She remembered Major Bethill and his love-making not three weeks ago. "He told me he loved me, and now he is engaged to another girl. Is she fancying he loves her, as I was fancying just now that Hamilton loved me? Are all men like this, and are we all poor deluded fools?"

Bethill's conduct, by a strange recoil of feeling on Ada's part, affected his rival; too young to feel confidence in her own experience, her own feelings, she placed exaggerated faith in the experience of others. And had not every author, every poet, told of the proverbial inconstancy of men; was it all true, did passion with them mean a bright fleeting fancy? When women listened to their promises and vows, did they in every instance meet with inconstancy and change?

And Ada thought, with a good sense, and justice, which was perhaps the peculiar character of her mind, that if it was so, men were not perhaps to blame, and women should learn to expect and bear it. " I would never weary my husband with prayer or entreaty if once I saw he had changed towards me, I would try to be his friend as a man would be ; men have friends amongst each other—I would offer him my friendship, I would never offer my love ; is that how some husbands and wives are happy, for some are —the most determined upholders of the theory that love never lasts, cannot last, admit there have been strongly attached husbands and wives. Is this the secret, or is the love that poets describe, novelists, some of them, speak of, is it a reality, and is it as they say, immortal ? Was Byron right! would he have lived and died happy and unknown had he been married to the woman whom he said he could have loved? Is that Dante's, Tasso's story, or should they have been like Milton, soon tired of the fancied prize when won ; but there have been others beside Milton. Did Abelard tire of Eloisa—he was a monk," she said, laughing, "that is not a fair instance. Petrarch, too, could not tire of Laura, she was never his. It seems as if it were so, indeed, as if none of these men could be constant—Dante marries— Byron marries—Petrarch and Tasso, they were never married ; they, too, tell us love is immortal, and they are perhaps more worthy to be heard, as they do not themselves supply the instance to the contrary : but why should we for ever hear that such is life, if it be false ? Why would men ever describe each other as changeable and fickle if it is not so? And what a fate, to love, and to find oneself

Major Bethill's wife; for when once a woman has married, life is lost to her if she has made a mistake; is it not better to try and turn one's heart to ambition, and worldly prosperity; if this is to be the end of love, is it not far better never to love? I suppose," the girl sadly thought, "it is our weakness makes us value affection so much, but it is not—not once in hundreds, that one can meet real love; and then, ought we not try and live without it? I have never loved, let me never dream of love, and if years hence I think of marrying, let it be some one whose character I well know; who, though he will never love or understand me, will at least be a good-natured, kind friend: that is the safest, wisest, course for me. I would be vain and foolish if I had inspired the attachment I have seen pictured in these reveries of mine; I would wake up a deluded fool, conscious of my egregious blunder, and resenting the deception which had been practised on me. And if I marry, let it be someone who has not deceived me, at all events; someone who will take me as his friend, without despising me for having been his dupe. Since I am unfortunately one of those women who could value love, real love, I am incapable of being happy except through two chances, the great chance of meeting such an affection as I have dreamt of, or the smaller chance," said she, smiling bitterly, "of falling into the hands of someone who did not at least mean to deceive me, and who, when his fancy for me is gone, will yet let me be his friend as far as we can be friends. It's a poor chance; better be alone, an old friendless woman." And again the girl's tears dropped hot and fast upon her hands; but she roused herself from this depression, she walked to the window. "It is dark and cold, but I will walk up and down for a time, it will cure me of this folly," and she put on her hat and walked up and down the gravel walks near the house, until her spirits seemed to have recovered and her depression passed away.

In the evening, her aunt laughed and chatted with her about the Hamiltons; was Mrs. Alton perfectly blind to Edmund's attachment?

Ada could not say; if she was not, she acted with extreme good sense—she neither praised, nor blamed, nor alluded to him, except by saying she liked the Hamiltons; she laughed over Major Bethill's engagement, and when Ada said—

"He is a strange lover, when three weeks ago he was a beau of mine."

Her aunt again laughed. "My dear," said

she, " he is very likely to be exceedingly well suited in his wife, she has some money, and that suits him ; he has a respectable position, that suits her."

" But, aunt, she may **be** greatly deceived in **him ; she may think he** cares for her, which is impossible."

" Ada dear, she **is** very safe, depend on **it ;** women know love when they are capable of **feeling** it—know it very well ; and, when they are not, they know a match that suits them, that is my experience for you."

" You don't think women are often deceived aunt—in love, I mean ?" Ada said, blushing.

" Very seldom, I think ; say what you will, **Ada,** women are not what men—and books are chiefly written by men—lead one to imagine. Now and then you meet a high-minded man, and his counterpart among women—your mother was one—but the idea that men are wolves and women lambs, is quite contrary to my experience."

"You don't think," said Ada, "that all books say about men's ingratitude and inconstancy is true?"

"I think a book which makes an impression on one, a book written by a superior man, reflects his mind Ada. He is disgusted at cruelty and injustice; he brands with his own contempt the cruelty and injustice he has seen practised around him by lower natures than his own; this is why men rail at the cruelty and inconstancy of men; women who have more sensibility than the common average of women, do the same, speaking of women— they are neither of them to be believed, they take a partial view of life; there are as high-minded men as women, and women as men, but one cannot expect to meet many of either, as they are a small proportion amongst the mass."

"But, aunt, do not some **men** treat women with great ingratitude?"

"Ingratitude, indeed," said her aunt, "**grateful for** having a trap laid for him? **what else are** half **the** women doing but setting traps for men? and when one escapes, **they set** up a scream enough to pierce ones **ears.** If, my dear, you allude to bad women —unfortunate victims as the papers call them —they are **the** greatest schemers of all, scheming **on the** man's marrying them at last, to avoid scandal, or their getting a large sum **of** money from him; no, dear, men may believe these tales—no woman of fifty ever yet believed them; and, Ada, girls like you should not waste your pity on such characters."

Ada smiled, her heart was not saddened by this picture of her sex; quite the reverse, she seemed to accept it as a pleasing one.

I am inclined to think that Mrs. Alton was a remarkably shrewd old lady, and that her own experience of life was not such as to lead her into thinking it desirable that her niece should be an old maid, or remain in ignorance of life as it really is.

As Ada kissed her and bade her good-night, her aunt smiled kindly.

"You are looking so well to-day, Ada, dear," said she. "You won't be long in taking Charlie's heart."

Ada was pleased, but in her eyes hearts were far more serious matters than in her aunt's.

" He is a sailor," said Mrs. Alton, with her good-humoured laugh; " he will make love to every woman he meets."

CHAPTER XIV.

COLONEL AND MRS. TRAVERS had come to The Grange on a visit, and Harriet and her mother were seated in the drawing-room. Harriet was very handsomely dressed, and was looking very well; she had been asking her mother many particulars about Harry's marriage. Colonel Travers had gone out fishing with the two Hamiltons.

" And, Harriet, how do you like your new house—is it a good one ?" said Mrs. Hamilton.

" It is very well, it is in a nice domain, and it is a large house ; but it wants to be newly furnished, it is full of rubbish brought from India—Indian this and that, curiosities they say ;—I don't like them, and I will have it all changed some of these days."

" And the neighbourhood—is it good ? have you been out much ?"

" Very little : it is a bad place I am afraid for Alice. I will never get her off my hands there ; I have been thinking what I ought to do."

" She has time enough yet," said Mrs. Hamilton.

" Oh ! the sooner the better, mamma."

" She and I may not be always such friends. There are very few people near us that seem to me likely to suit her, no one in fact ; there is a clergyman, an old widower— Alice has not my fancy for old widowers, I can see—and a doctor, who has sometimes attended the Colonel."

" And the servants—are they good ones? do you like them ?"

" They are not very good, I think ; some of them have been there for ages, and of course have given up doing anything, as all old family servants do. There is an old nurse, or housekeeper; she is a great nuisance, she directed everything: of course, Alice was a mere child, but I will send her off, I really could not put up with her now."

" Is she a favourite with them at Horton ?" said her mother.

" The greatest you can imagine, mamma ; they have been all spoiled by her. She nursed the children, and attended Mrs. Travers for years before her death : the Colonel tells me his wife asked him to keep her always about the place—did you ever hear of such a thing ?

He quite thinks she ought to remain on because of that. It just shows me what a wily,
designing woman she is to have managed so
well for herself."

Mrs. Hamilton asked her age.

"Oh! she is old—seventy, or near seventy,
I should think."

"She won't live long, then, Harriet, dear."

"Long! oh, long enough, I daresay—too
long to wait at all events—why she might live
these ten years, and is likely to live for the
next five at least. Oh, no, I must get rid of
her, however I manage it."

"Is Alice a clever girl?" said Mrs. Hamilton, changing the subject.

"They say she is : she sings very well, but
does not play or draw. I hear she is clever;
she writes very amusing letters—she wrote to
her father every week—she is droll; she has
a good figure, and dresses well enough, but

she is plain—very, I think. Don't you remember my showing you her—oh, I forgot,
you saw her of course—what do you think
yourself?"

"I think as you say, she is no beauty: I
meant, was she a pleasant person to live
with?"

"She is exceedingly civil to me, and very
fond of the Colonel, and he is very fond of
her I think; but she seldom talks to me, I
can't make her out, I suppose she dislikes
me."

"Oh! Harriet, why think such a thing? if
she is civil and good-natured, what more need
you want or expect?"

"I expect to get her married, my good
mother; will you find me a husband for her?
I do not intend to ask for Edmund, so you
need not start—by-the-bye, how does the
Lowell affair get on?"

"I do not think anything has changed; he seems to pay her as great attention as ever, but never talks of her to me, even in the most casual way. I wonder would Mrs. Alton object or approve."

"Hardly approve, though who knows: Edmund is a good fellow, and some people think very clever. Mrs. Alton, I believe, likes all that, but I fancy she would expect something greater for Ada—she will have plenty of money, will she not, mother?"

"I daresay her aunt might give her, or leave her, a couple of thousand a year: there is a nephew of hers coming home—Charlie Domville, you remember—perhaps she would wish to get them married."

"A very handsome little fellow! very dark, with curly hair, is that he?"

"Yes—he is about four-and-twenty now, and they say very handsome, and I daresay

Mrs. Alton would wish to have them married, or she would not let him come. I think myself Ada is a strange girl, and will surprise her aunt yet by some foolish match."

" And so Edmund says Harry's wife is quite a Frenchwoman !"

" Oh ! quite—can't bear this country, and has such a French manner. Edmund did not admire her; he says she is very much admired, she is a great dasher, and so extravagant. I suppose they will not live at the Manor much."

"Not they, I suppose," said Harriet. " She will run off with one of these Frenchmen sooner or later, I daresay."

" Very likely," said Mrs. Hamilton, quite placidly. These things did not ruffle her; she had seen some such events occur in her own little world, and after a time they had been forgotten: but they were matters which she thought should enter into calculations extending over any lengthened period of time, at least as possibilities. " I should not be at all surprised if it were so," she said.

" This is all imagination, mother; she is nothing more than a pretty little girl, with a French air about her. Edmund has prejudiced you, he is full of fancies. But what do you think of Alice? of her marrying, I mean ?"

" I really can't say, Harriet."

" Should I not try and get her settled as soon as possible ? What do you think of the widower for her—he is a rich old clergyman ?"

" She would not like that, perhaps, and the Colonel might think it too precipitate. Wait a little, dear, and entertain; you will soon find some one for her, depend on it."

" She does not care in the least to set herself off. I should not be surprised by her
ending in marrying the doctor."

" Is he a young man ?"

" He is a good-looking, stupid young man ;
very hard working, and very badly dressed."

" You should try and get the Colonel to
employ some one else : tell him what you
suspect, and I am sure he will at once."

But Harriet laughed. " Not he," she said ;
" he would only think me suspicious, and not
sufficiently inclined to believe in what he calls
Alice's perfect openness of character. Here
they are coming in !"

Colonel Travers said they had been very
successful ; they had caught three trout—
very small ones, indeed—but it was too bright,
and he considered it a great proof of his skill
having succeeded in taking any. Fred, who
seldom went out, gave a ludicrous description

of the day's sport—the cold, the half-dozen
times the hook caught in trees and weeds, and
the intense excitement when the first little
sprat was hauled in until his size was clearly
seen, then their disgust—" And the whole
time, whenever I spoke, I was told I had
frightened the fish out of the river. I hope
we won't have any of this sort of thing at
Sefton. I hear Domville has come."

" Yes," said Colonel Travers, " we met
Mr. Sandford—a very nice person, indeed;
your rector, I believe, Mrs. Hamilton—h e
told us that young Domville had arrived."

" I expected he would have been here to-
day, to call on you, Colonel Travers."

" Sandford made me many apologies when
I met him."

" Edmund, did you catch anything ?"

" Nothing, Harriet; my luck was very

bad. I lost the entire casting line, a most stupid thing."

"How you like it I cannot imagine; it is so slow and solitary, and so wretched, as the weather ought to be cloudy and no sun ; one always hears it is too clear or too bright."

"I must say," said Edmund, "I prefer a day's hunting ; it it more exciting, and there is some society."

" Fishing is a nice amusement for a clergy-man—fishing and photography. I wonder Sandford does not adopt either," said Fred.

" The worst of photography is, you are asked to take likenesses. The pretty child of the family, the pet horse, or dog, must have its carte ; and if it's not sufficiently flattering, you lose your parishioners, and if you refuse, you are thought little better than a churl."

" Did you see Harriet's last, Mrs. Hamilton? It was taken while we were in Paris, and is very good."

"They don't want another of me in this house," said Harriet.

"I will show you a beautiful one of Mrs. Lawson. I have it somewhere in my desk; it is in evening dress. I will bring it down in the evening, if I can find it," said Edmund.

In looking for it, Edmund pulled out his desk from side to side, but could not remember where he had laid the photograph. In doing so, two small gold coins fell out; he caught them, brought them nearer the light, and walked to the fire with them. He seemed inclined to throw them in. As he bent over the fire, he said—

"It would be better, no doubt; but they can't recall her more than everything else does."

And he moved **away again** from the fire, and after folding them up in some fresh paper, **put** them back **again** in their old position. **A** queer, unexplained fancy had crossed his mind.

" If **I** were superstitious, I would fancy that something **they** told me; I would yet give her those coins. I am superstitious, for I will keep **them**," he thought.

He laughed at himself a few moments later, for being influenced by such an idea, and told himself it was **better to** accept **the** truth at once that Ada had tried to impart, and act on the implied compact which existed between them when she offered him her hand and he bid her good-bye.

CHAPTER XV.

It was breakfast hour at Horton, the name of Colonel Travers's place ; but there was no one but Alice Travers at breakfast. She was sitting in a very pretty morning room, the walls of which were covered with prints; she had let the breakfast things lie on the table, though she had long since finished hers. She was not a handsome girl, but her face was pleasant and expressive. She held a letter in her hand.

An old woman, respectably dressed, came in ; she walked up to the tea table.

"You have not eaten anything, miss, although you were down so early."

"No, nurse, I can't eat; here is a letter from Mrs. Travers. She says they won't come home for another week, and that she wishes you to get the room over the hall ready; her brother is coming back with them."

"The young gentleman was here last time, miss."

"No, her eldest brother; she seems very particular about him, nurse. Oh, dear, what shall I do to-day."

"Well, miss, why not go out and take a ride; you would be the better for it, I am sure."

"I am the better of nothing, nurse; I have got a disease called *ennui*. Did you ever hear of it in India?"

"I don't remember, miss; but you look seemingly very well."

" That's it; that is one of the worst symptoms. What shall I do?"

" Might I take a liberty, miss; might I speak quite freely to you, and you not be offended?"

" Speak away, nurse; the worst of it is, I have not life enough now to be offended the way I used."

" Well, my darling, listen to an old woman —a poor old woman who wishes you well, and would not but wish your mother's daughter well. She was a dear woman, your mother was; and, miss, don't now be going walking about with that young doctor from the village."

" Is it Dr. Johnston, nurse?" said Alice, colouring.

" Yes, miss, the doctor," said the old nurse; " he is not fit for the like of you—a fine

young lady—and it's making little of yourself going and meeting him, and walking up
and down the avenue with him, as I hear."

"You are right enough," said Alice, " I
know I ought not ; but I have an awful life
here—I have, indeed—everything is so
changed since you and I were managing,
nurse.   Did I ever then do these things ? was
I not as gay as could be ? and spent the day
looking over the flowers, and garden, and
house, and riding about?   I did not walk
with the doctor then—did I now, nurse ?"

"Not as I know, miss, and that's what sur-
prises me now."

" Because, my good old woman," said the
girl, passionately, "I had other hopes, and
ideas, and employments then,—dare I touch
the flowers now ? dare I tell the gardener to
do this or that? dare I settle what was to be
done in the house, or that I would drive the

ponies, or ride the grey? No—whatever I would propose to do now would be wrong. I can choose my own dresses, that's nearly all I can do—but how am I to live this life—I tell you I can't nurse—and no wonder I walk and talk with that poor stupid doctor, who thinks I am an angel, and listens to me abusing every one. I would not be bored with his love, nurse, don't think it."

"Ah! but, my dear miss, it's little matter; the world will soon hear you walk with him, and who will believe he is not your lover, and then you are ruined—you are, my darling, and you that's so clever, and such a real lady," and the poor old woman wiped her eyes. "And now you will be angry, I am sure, miss," she continued: "but if you would just wait a bit, you might meet some nice young gentleman you would like; may-be this Mr. Hamilton—they tell me he is a fine gentleman, something like what you used to tell me long ago you'd have for your lover."

" Did I ?" said Alice.   "What did I say ?"

" You said you liked a fair-haired gentle-man, miss; that's what I was thinking of when I was asking about young Mr. Hamilton."

" Oh ! nurse—what folly !   He is just like Mrs. Travers, I am sure, and I never could like her; you know I did not like her officer brother who was here."

" Brothers is very different, miss;   and don't now, my own darling, be meeting that Doctor Johnston."

" Well, I won't, if it annoys you, nurse: I don't care if I never saw him again— I don't, upon my word," she said.

" God grant it, miss, that's all I say; it would be a poor thing to be deceiving a poor old creature only who wishes you well."

" I don't deceive any one—not you, certainly, nurse—but you ought to pity me. Do
you know what Mrs. Travers said to me the
last time that she was at home?—she said, ' I
wish I saw you married to that dear old Mr.
Lloyd.' The horrid old creature! I'll never
marry him."

" No, you won't dear ; you will marry her
own brother, perhaps, and be a great lady—
a greater lady than she, and you will have a
handsome place—and she will be jealous of
you yet, for you will have money, and beauty,
and all she would wish for—you will, darling."

" Very well, I have no objection; but it
seems to me it's a castle in the air, rather—
however, I don't object, nurse, remember
that."

The old woman took up the tea tray, and

put the things aside; and as she went away, she said—

"Now, like a dear lady, when that gentleman comes, put on your rings, and your jewellery, and your nice dress, and see if what I tell you is not the wisest thing."

"Yes, yes," said the girl, "of course;" and when the old nurse had gone, she began laughing. "What a poor good old creature she is; and how she is fretting about the doctor. I daresay I will give up seeing him; it's beneath me, as she says. And what do I do it for? she wants me to set my cap at Mr. Hamilton, that's her advice. Well, we will see."

A week had passed, Colonel and Mrs. Travers had come, and Edmund also; and the old nurse's advice had been taken; and Alice dressed herself becomingly and received the parties with the gayest smiles; and now it was the day after, and she and Edmund were going out to ride. As Edmund put her on her horse he thought of Ada, and the contrast in appearance was not favourable to Alice; but as they rode along, and chatted over many things, Edmund admitted she was intelligent, and agreeable; she was very plain though, he thought; but for her good figure she would be quite commonplace, but she was a graceful bold rider.

"You are very fond of riding are you not, Mr. Hamilton?"

"I am very; I hunt a great deal. Have you ever seen a good run?"

"I have once or twice, but I was driving, and could not see much; I should think it was a very pleasant thing to ride to a meet."

"If you come to us in winter I will bring you out, and show you all I can."

"You are very, very kind to me. You know I am very lonely here now. When papa was unmarried I managed everything; it is very different. Papa does not want me now, and I don't often go out," she said, blushing.

Edmund suspected his sister was not a very considerate stepmother. He pitied Alice.

"You must feel it very much," he said. "I wish you had some society. If you were near us I would bring you out as often as you wished. Are you fond of reading?"

"I read a great deal—novels and poetry, and all that I can lay my hands on, in fact. Do you read novels?" she said.

"Indeed, I do; too many I am afraid. And what do you like in a novel; do you like Scott, and those worthies?"

"I don't, indeed; though I tell papa I have read them all; I have only skipped

through them. I don't like any of Scott's,
except 'Kenilworth'—not 'Ivanhoe,' even.
Papa was quite offended when I said so."

"Why, it is the one most admired; don't
you like Rebecca?"

"Yes; but I don't like 'Ivanhoe'—is he
not something like De Wilton, in 'Marmion?'"

"I don't remember him," said Edmund;
"but Scott always makes his heroes contemptible, I think. He liked the unsuccess-
ful lovers far better; he was identifying
himself with 'Marmion' and Bois Guilbert,
perhaps."

"Yes, so I saw in some book; because he
had been himself unfortunate in love—was
not that it? but he was married, and had
forgotten."

"He was married, but he had not forgotten;
that seems about the real state of things,
eh?"

" How horrid it must be to think one was married in that way; don't you think so, Mr. Hamilton?"

" That your husband, or wife, had been in love before?   Yes; one would not choose it, not when one is young, but they are very happy often.   You may meet a person who is more worthy of being loved, perhaps, afterwards; do you think that could be?"

" I should not care; I should still wish to be the first.   Who is your favourite hero, Mr. Hamilton?"

" I think I like Tennyson's Lancelot in the ' Idyls.' "

" I like that book greatly; poor Elaine. But I was glad he let her die; were you when you read it?"

" Oh, yes! that is the whole romance of the tale; but for that it would resemble some novels I have read where there are two heroines, and you cannot discover which the hero is in love with until the last page."

"I did not 'like Enid; Geraint seemed to me such a savage; he treated her so cruelly, and made her so ridiculous—driving the horses. I would never forgive that."

"He was jealous, you must remember," said Edmund, who thought a good deal might be excused when this was the case.

"Oh! I could not excuse that, Mr. Hamilton, jealous or not."

"You should, though; think what it is to fancy you were married in that way, as you said yourself."

"Yes," said Alice; "but it seems so cruel in a strong man."

"A strong man, perhaps, feels as much as the weakest woman, if he feels at all."

"Now could you have treated Enid so, Mr. Hamilton?"

" Not," said Hamilton, laughing, " if you were Enid."

" Shall we have a canter," said Alice, blushing.

They chatted on of many things. Edmund told her of the foreign towns he had seen and life abroad, and she was such an interested listener he talked more and more. Alice had a quick tact; she read Edmund's character; saw he was very different from her step-mother; and she was soon at her ease with him, and he liked and pitied her. They went out every day to ride, and every day the rides were longer and longer. The day before Edmund intended leaving they had ridden to some ruins, which, as the old servant held their horses, they walked round.

" What a lovely place for a pic-nic. We must get Harriet to give us one in summer, it is cold yet; but I will show you a prettier ruin when you come to us."

" When will that be?" he said.

" Oh, as soon as your sister will go. I shall be so delighted to see all the places you tell me of."

" And," Edmund said, " perhaps we could get Ada—I mean Miss Lowell—to come with us."

" Who is she?" said Alice, who thought their rides could not be improved on.

" She is a young lady who lives near us; she rides a great deal."

" Have you often ridden with her?"

" Very often, indeed."

It seemed to Alice that all pleasure had suddenly departed from her anticipated excursions with him, since he wished to have some additional society. Since it was his habit to ride with other young ladies she felt

she would sooner be at home. As they returned she was sad and depressed. Edmund
did not see it, or attributed it to her being
somewhat tired; but as she took off her habit
and hat she said, laughing, to the old nurse—

" Nurse, I am fated to be an humble imita-
tion of Elaine."

" What," said the old nurse.

" Oh, nurse ! it is well you don't see all the
mischief you have done. Good-night, for I
must go down to dinner, and I won't see you
again this evening."

CHAPTER XVI.

ALICE sang, so did Harriet; they generally sang every evening; and since Edmund came Harriet had been very gay and good-humoured, sitting at the piano and singing song after song as Edmund asked for them, leaving Alice and he to entertain each other. Sometimes Alice sang, and then, indeed, Edmund was delighted. She had a lovely voice. She sang with an amount of taste and feeling which is very rare; and, perhaps, in some of her songs her own feelings may have in some degree found expression. It was unlike any other singing Edmund had heard, and he listened with the greatest pleasure, and expressed the greatest admiration.

"You never play any of the good old music," he said, one day; "how is this?"

"I only care to sing," she said. "I cannot play more than an accompaniment."

"You sing so well—yours is so different from Harriet's singing, I never asked her to sing till I came here; I only asked her to hear you."

Alice blushed; she had forgotten Elaine, for Edmund had stayed two days longer than he had intended, and he had on those evenings again and again asked her to sing. Harriet had returned into the dining room, where the old Colonel generally sat sipping his wine alone, and Edmund said, as Alice concluded her song—

" That song always reminds me of a lady I know; she has just such eyes as you are singing about."

A sharp pang ran through Alice's heart. " Who is this lady; is she the Ada he mentioned before," Alice thought; she only said, " Yes, is it not a very good description of handsome eyes ; but I don't generally like a song describing any person."

" Oh, no. One is tired of hearing of raven and golden tresses, and all that sort of rubbish, I shall not hear such singing again for a long time."

" Are you going to-morrow ?"

" Oh, yes, to-morrow; my brother will be off, and I must see him before he goes. I have been here longer than I intended; I hope you and Harriet will soon come over. I will ride with you every morning, if you will promise to sing for me in the evening; will you agree to that?"

"I delight in singing for anyone who really likes hearing me. Sometimes I know I am only asked because it is considered civil; then I can't bear having to sing, or when there is a large party."

"Just so," said Harriet, who then entered the room. "I could not induce her to sing at the last party we had here, and I wished her to make an impression on the heart of a gentleman who seemed to me a little attracted by her; but she told me that she hated widowers."

"Yes, indeed, I said so," said Alice; "but you know some people have that feeling. I see now how rude it was, but I never meant it as a rudeness."

Edmund laughed.

"It is very natural she should feel and

speak in that way, I think, Harriet," Edmund said.

"Oh! I see, you will defend anything she says or does; but I thought it foolish, for he would have been a very good match," and Harriet walked out of the room.

"How horridly unsentimental she is," said her brother; "everything seems doubly hard and hollow, and contemptible, when one is talking to her of it. I never could get on with her, or my brother Fred; not that we quarrel, but we can't understand each other. Fred is good natured, though he would do me a good turn, as he would say, but he would laugh at me all the time."

You see Edmund and Alice had become very friendly and confidential; was Edmund beginning to follow the old and approved course; was he to find forgetfulness where so

many have found it, in a new excitement;
had Alice's flattering attention to his wishes
and opinions, that perfectly innocent and
truthful admiration, not been without its own
subtle charm?   Was he beginning to feel
that Ada's retiring, half-timid coldness was
not after all the strongest spell?—that a
woman might also win love by an utterly
opposite attraction.

As yet I can only say he had never compared them, except to wish his Ada beside
him, to fancy how happy he might be sitting
in those May evenings at her feet; to wander
off into reveries, in which he explained away
her conduct to him by saying she was not in
love with anyone. There was now no Bethill
to compete for her smiles—Bethill had been
discarded; and though as yet she had not
loved him, he would be her lover, and her
lover only all his life, and she would yet be

his. He had been foolish, precipitate; he had frightened her from him. But she had a heart to appeal to—a heart which could recognise his devotion; it was still hers to give, and his to gain. And he gazed on the beautiful lights and shadows thrown by the moonlight on the park and its trees with the softest and most sentimental air, as Alice's voice rose and fell in its rich soft cadence; and as she glanced at him from behind her cottage piano, she could not but admire his handsome, earnest face; while he, as she gazed, rapt in his reverie, pictured her rival —whom he loved—in all her well remembered beauty.

And something of this dimly, and indistinctly, and half-blinded by her hopes as she was, Alice could still suspect. She did not think he loved her; this is not the way in which people throw away their hearts. No, she only thought that he was all she could love, and that yet he might, perhaps, forget her being plain and unattractive, and love her for her heart and mind, and for the love she bore him ; for poor Alice fancied her face was not fair enough to win any man's love, except inch by inch as it were. She attributed Edmund's perfect ease of manner, his frankness and kindness in speaking to her, to their true origin—his indifference; but she imagined this was only because she was not all which his fancy had pictured the woman he could admire should be. The eyes which her song described—those were the eyes he could have sworn he loved; had she beauty such as that, she thought he would have been even now beside her, telling her she was an angel, and an enchantress, as poor Doctor Johnston did. She forgot that at no period had that poor deluded mortal, Doctor Johnston, considered her other than an angel, an enchantress, and that reasoning from that instance, if Edmund were ever to think her such, he would have probably done so from the first.

This reflection did not occur to her; on the contrary, she recalled her father's marriage, and that evidently its only cause was Harriet's beauty. In nothing was Mrs. Travers what her father had asserted to Alice he loved in women—what he said he hoped his daughter would become. "And so it is," she thought, "with Edmund. I am not what he admires; he only likes me as his friend and companion, and it must be slowly —very slowly, I shall gain his heart; and if, like my father, he meets one whom he can admire, I shall be for ever forgotten. Poor Elaine! will her fate be mine. And

then she thought Edmund was far more clear
sighted than her father; he would be able to
read the character of such a woman as her
stepmother—he would not marry such a
person.   It was only the union of beauty,
with every qualification which he admired,
that she feared; and that perfect creature he
was not likely to meet, who would be able to
replace her as his friend and companion,
while she outshone all others as a beauty.
He will fancy he will meet her, and then
having seen many beauties whom he cannot
admire, he will find, perhaps, that he prefers
me; and that in my case will be the course
of true love," Alice whispered to herself.

Had she known the truth, would she have
still deceived herself?   This is a difficult
question to answer; I almost might venture
to say she would not, but who can exactly

predict the beatings of even one human heart?
Has it not mysteries and aspirations which
we can never divine—wild hopes and sorrows
known only to itself?

Harriet came in and called for candles
immediately, and tea was got ready; and
Edmund ceased to see Ada's figure between
him and the large beech tree. Indeed, a
good inch board intervened now in the shape
of a shutter, and Harriet gave him messages
to her mother, and little presents for Fred,
which had all to be remembered and taken
proper care of, for he was to leave before the
ladies came down the following morning.

But after the Colonel and Alice had left,
Harriet said, bidding her brother good-bye—

" You have evidently made a conquest
here, Edmund. Do you intend to have a
second string to your bow, in case the fair

Ada is not to be had? or is it mere vanity makes you bewitch my daughter? If so, I must tell the Colonel."

"Bewitched," said Edmund, laughing, "I am sure you can see yourself how little bewitched I am; but she is a nice girl, and I really like her."

"I did not say you were bewitched, my friend—merely that you have bewitched the girl; that's plain enough, I should think, and I expect you will marry her, if you don't get Ada. That's not being hard on you, is it now?"

"Marry her!" exclaimed Edmund; but whatever he had intended saying he stopped, and ended by—"You are a great match maker, Harriet; good night. You need not fret about her; she is heart whole, and so am I."

" The one is as true as the other," said Harriet, as she closed the door, leaving Edmund with the impression she had rather the best of that discussion.

CHAPTER XVII.

FRED started to join his regiment amidst
many tears from his mother and good wishes
from his brothers; the boys having had a
week's holiday to come home and see him off.
He was rather a favourite with his father,
who displayed his regret at his leaving by
giving Fred a hundred pound note for pocket
money, when he went into his room to bid
him good-bye before he left. Poor Mr.
Hamilton was suffering terribly from rheu-
matism, and was in a state of great depression
after a night of torture.

"Take care of yourself, Fred, and try and avoid this awful complaint; I am fit for Bedlam to day. I feel I could run a knife into it," he said, looking viciously at his leg, which was lying in state on a down cushion; "it's worse than gout, for it's far more constant. Good-bye, Fred—God bless you. Write for your allowance; I may forget it with this infernal torture. Don't play cards, and keep clear of the Jews. It's better now—good-bye. Don't come too close."

Fred shook hands, and Mr. Hamilton relapsed into his lamentations after he had gone; he really suffered dreadfully, and looked like a spectre after a fortnight or so of these sufferings, which with him were spasmodic at times in their intensity.

Edmund and his brother separated with very little profession on either side. "Good-bye, old fellow."

"Good-bye, Ned, exercise Grouse yourself for me," and the brothers had parted.

When Edmund had returned from rambling about the place, seeing how the horses and dogs had been treated during his absence, his mother gave him a note.

"This came a day or two ago, Edmund, but I did not forward it; I think they had a croquet party at Sefton; I suppose it was for that."

"Yes, mother, I had promised to go over and call on young Domville; I must go—the croquet party is past; I see it was on the sixth. Were they here since?"

"No, they were not; I must go to your father, he is not at all well to-day.

"I must go and see them and this cousin too; I wonder what he is like, now; they never had the meet at Sefton that we spoke of. I must tell Ada fortune decided that in my favour. I think I will ride over there to-day and see what is doing," Edmund thought.

Edmund rode over, but he saw no one stirring about, as he walked his horse up the avenue. When he asked for Mrs. Alton and Mr. Domville, he was told she and Miss Lowell were out driving, and Mr. Domville was somewhere about the place. As he was riding away he heard some one calling after him; he turned round, and Domville jumped out of the drawing-room window, and was beside him in a moment.

"Just saw your card in time, Hamilton," he said; "I am so glad I did come in; the ladies are out, but they told me you were coming to see me some day. It's a charity; this is an awful stupid place, only for Ada I don't think I could stand it long."

Hamilton came in, and they arranged to meet and go out fishing together in a stream, about two miles from Sefton. "Not," as Domville explained, "that he cared a hang for fishing, but it would kill a day."

Domville was a very good looking little fellow, rather small, dark, and curly haired, with a restless, lively, good-natured manner; you felt you knew him at once. He told Hamilton how old he was, how many cigars he generally smoked, and how much he liked the sea; that this was a very jolly place, if he only had some fellow to talk to, and that he would go over and see Hamilton the next day, and ended by having one of the horses saddled, and riding back with Edmund part of the way.

"I wish Fred was at home, he would be a great companion for this fellow," thought Hamilton. "I never could amuse him; he wants so much amusing; I will try and get Sandford's son to come out with us to-morrow, if any one would amuse him he ought; they are something like."

Domville was over next day, as he had said, but he did not require as much amusing as Edmund had feared; on the contrary he seemed to amuse himself greatly to Edmund's satisfaction, and was full of good spirits and good humour. He told Edmund that they had had an engagement with a Chillian vessel, and that he had saved two sailor's lives—he did not say how. "And I am trying to get a Victoria Cross. I have written to my uncle; he is a Member of Parliament, and they say that is the way to go about it, and I might get it with a little interest; you know it is a great thing to have—not that either, for twenty fellows did more—but you see my cousin Ada would like it I am sure. Women do always, don't they? She is a very pretty girl, is she not?"

Hamilton did not like these confidences very much, we may be sure, but they could not be avoided. Whatever Domville was thinking of he talked of.

Hamilton went over to Sefton a few days after to fish ; he and Ada met just as usual ; he tried to observe how she and her cousin got on, but Domville kept up such a constant conversation with him, he could not remark anything in particular—he dined there, and he thought, as he brought in Ada to dinner, that she was gayer than usual—he was to a certain degree right. She had feared that Edmund and she would not again meet as friends, and when they met, and he was attentive and kind, and devoted as ever, the apprehension which had weighed on her spirits seemed gone. Never had Edmund seen her so gay ; she laughed and chatted, and her aunt, who seemed exceedingly interested in some of Charlie's adventures, left Edmund and her completely to themselves, but he did not revert in any way to their previous conversation; and in this I think he showed some judgment.

They strolled through the grounds after dinner. Charlie, in the most amusing way, having said—so that Ada most probably heard him—" Take care of my aunt like a good fellow, while I have a chat with my cousin."

Edmund could not refuse such a request, and had the satisfaction of a long conversation with Mrs. Alton, who, though an exceedingly agreeable woman, was not, I am afraid, as well able to excite his interest by her conversational powers as Alice Travers.

" You are a good fellow," said Charlie, when they had all entered the house. " I can only say I will do as much for you any day."

Edmund laughed. " What are you laughing at, Mr. Hamilton?" said Ada.

"An offer your cousin has made me; he can tell you about it himself;" and he probably did so, Edmund afterwards thought.

"I had a letter from your sister Mrs. Travers," said Ada, in the course of the evening. "She tells me she intends paying you a visit, and bringing her step-daughter. I shall go over and see her when she comes, but she has forgotten to mention the day; and I'll bring the flowers she asks for."

"I have not heard when she is coming, but I shall let you hear if she comes suddenly; we did not expect her for a month."

This was all Edmund said on the subject; but why had he a nervous dread of his sister's corresponding with Ada? He had this dread, for he knew of old how meddlesome and mischievous Harriet was, and feared she had some schemes in connection with Alice and himself which he did not quite see through.

CHAPTER XVIII.

HARRIET being impatient to realize her plans, determined to pay The Grange a visit immediately, bringing Alice with her, who was by no means averse. Indeed Alice felt the house more lonely than ever after Edmund's departure, and when her old nurse—sitting by the fire in her room—talked of him, praising him of course, and assuring her that it was evident to every one how much he admired her, though she punctiliously contradicted the assertion whenever made; still we may be sure it did not displease or surprise her.

"I have got a letter for you, miss," said the old nurse—Alice's face flushed crimson—with that tact which we so often see brought to wonderful perfection in the bearing of our inferiors, and which perhaps to some minds, is one reason their society is too attractive—the nurse in saying this, busied herself bringing Alice her brushes and combs, and seemed to have quite forgotten to observe how she received the intelligence.

"Where is it, nurse? It's from the doctor, of course?"

"Yes, miss, when you were going out to ride yesterday I got it; a messenger brought it. I knew him, and I said I was told to ask him for a note, which I saw he had; he said it was for the young lady, and he gave it to me."

"You did very right, nurse; I am obliged to you for this."

Alice took the letter and read it.

"MY OWN DEAR ALICE,

"How often within the last week have I waited and watched for you by the old yew tree; how anxiously I have listened for your footsteps. What is the reason? What have I done? How have I offended you? Of what have I been accused? If any one has accused me, Alice dear, give me an opportunity of defending myself. It is all I ask. See me once more—only once more.

"Your ever attached

"MAURICE."

I leave the reader to decide if this was not an embarrassing letter for a young lady who had fallen in love with another gentleman to receive; and as Alice read it she fully admitted how extremely disagreeable it was to have such an epistle addressed to her.

" One cannot forgive one's self for such weakness," she thought. "I have allowed this man to make love to me, now he takes the position of my accepted and acknowledged lover. What shall I do ?"

And then, through her remorse for having acted as she had towards Dr. Johnston, ran the lower feeling of dread of the consequences, should the existence of this lover ever become known to Edmund. She thought at once how his high wrought ideas and feelings would be revolutionised by such a discovery. She could not hope to be Elaine then in his eyes, but Vivian, perhaps, the wily and the false. In her extreme terror, for her feelings deserved no other name, she turned towards her nurse for such assistance as she could offer.

" What shall I do, nurse ?" And she read the letter.

Thus called into the counsels ot her mis-

tress, the old nurse was not without some re-
sources. Her first step was to take soundings,
as it were.

" Do you care for him, miss?" she said.

" Not a bit. I would be delighted to hear
he was married to-morrow. You may judge
how I care for him by that."

The nurse paused.

" Then, miss, we must only try and get rid
of him, and let him get married if he likes."

" Yes, of course; but that's the difficulty.
I don't know how to get rid of him, do
you?"

" Is he one of those men, miss, that's real
down right fond of those they take a fancy
to ? If he is, maybe it would be better to
pretend that you were prevented seeing him
by Mrs. Travers ; that she would have been
very angry if you had not gone out with her

brother; and that she had suspected something of your meetings, and you had to be very careful for the present. That would be the best thing to do, I think. He may, if he is very fond of you, come again and again, and write; and it may be known if you don't try to pacify him."

"And you think I should write. There is not one word of truth in all this, and he is so true and open, it's a shame to deceive him."

"You can't help him now, miss; he has been deceived long ago. The only thing now is to get out of it all friendly; it's a bad business."

"I think I will write, and you can send the letter for me."

"Oh! never fear, miss; I'll send the letter; but you would want to be very careful. If it's found out I am ruined altogether. Write it now, miss, while I am with you; indeed it is all you can do," she said, as Alice hesitated, bringing her paper and pens.

"You have the ink there, miss. Now do write and say you could not see him."

Alice took the pen from the old nurse's hand. All the meanness and duplicity of her conduct she fully acknowledged, and condemned too; but though she condemned herself, she saw no other escape from her position. "If Edmund should see or read this letter he will fancy I have loved this man, and he will never, never forgive me. I know he never will," she thought.

"Nurse," she said, "I am afraid to write. No one knows what may become of letters. Will you go to Doctor Johnston from me, and say that I was afraid to write to him, but that I have received his letter, and that I would have met him **only that** I was obliged to go out and ride with Mr. Hamilton."

Alice's face was crimson again. She suddenly hid it with her hands.

"It's too shameful," she **said.** "I had almost as **soon marry him.**"

The nurse faithfully **promised** to arrange the meeting safely.

"**I will go** and consult him, miss," she said, "about my eyes; that **will** be best. I can **get** leave from Mrs. Travers herself to go; and, indeed, I intended to go and see him about them."

Alice **listened with that** sickening at the details **of a** deception which we often retain after we **have** acknowledged to ourselves we are committed to a degrading course, while we are **yet** unwilling to dwell on it.

In her mind there was even for a moment or two a question as to whether **she** might not

as well end all her difficulties by marrying
the doctor; but the remembrance of Edmund
—Edmund, who was all she could admire—
decided her.

"No," she thought, "I would be wretched
if I fancied I might have been his wife, and
had married Doctor Johnston. No; I am
but carrying out an excusable deception. I
shall soon be able to confess the truth, and it
cannot now be helped, or anything better
done; though I do regret it all; though it is
a horrid shame."

The following evening the old nurse came
at the accustomed hour, when Alice was dressing for dinner, and Alice welcomed her with
great warmth.

"Tell me everything, nurse. What happened since?"

"I went to his house, miss, and asked to
see him, and was shown into the room he

sees the patients in, and I asked him about my eyes; and at first I was greatly confused thinking how I'd begin to speak to him, but as he was asking me had I long suffered with my eyes, I said, 'Oh! this long time, before I came to Horton with Colonel Travers.' And he then said, 'You are one of the servants, are you?' I told him I was; that I had seen him attending there, though he did not know me, and that I was your nurse; and had managed the house when master was a widower. He then asked me how you all were, and I began then, and told him you were not very well; that you were very much fretted by Mrs. Travers; that she was not kind to you. 'And now she is trying to get her married to Mr. Hamilton,' I said. He gave a start. 'Sir,' said I, 'the young lady sent me to speak to you.' 'Oh! did she?' he said. 'How good of you to take such trouble.'

And I said you were in dread of writing a letter, but that you would some of these days contrive to meet him at the same place, and I would bring him a message, and he would know all then from yourself; but that you told me nothing but that Mrs. Travers was very angry about your having been seen to meeʻ him; and then he asked me a great deal about you, and how you were, and did you fret, and not to let you fret at all if I could help it; and about Mr. Hamilton—was he a nice gentleman? and was he like Mrs. Travers? and what did the Colonel think? was he aware of it all? and a great deal more. Are you listening, miss?"

Alice was crying.

"Yes," she said, "yes, nurse, I am. I am very unhappy."

"Ah! then, is that you crying for that fellow, Miss Alice?"

" Oh ! it is such a shame; and I am afraid it will be found out."

" Not at all, miss; he is one of those men a child might deceive. He said he'd do anything you wished."

" You told him we were going to the Hamilton's, nurse, did you not?"

" Yes, miss; and he wrote you a letter, and gave it to me, with twenty charges, and made me eat my lunch, and took great care of me. Here it is ?"

And she gave Alice a letter, with a large dragon for a seal.

" My own dear Alice,—

" I am so delighted to hear all about you. You cannot think how unhappy I have been. I will do anything you wish me to do; you may rely upon that; but I would so much wish to meet you and talk all

this over.   Dear Alice, do see me once more.
I am so wretched, thinking you may forget
me.

" Ever your attached

" MAURICE."

Alice read the letter to her counsellor.

"You see, nurse, he still wants to see me.
What shall I do if I meet him.   I know, I'll
tell him the truth; I am sure I shall, though
I don't intend it."

"Oh ! miss, you'll be gone in a day or so.
What fear is there?   And don't be thinking
about the future; once you are engaged to
Mr. Hamilton what matter at all ?"

"But," said Alice, bitterly, "it is matter,
every matter.   He would not think of me if
he knew it ; and he is not thinking of me.
There is where you are quite wrong.   He has

N 5

paid me no attention. It is only that I like him, and now I have seen him I don't care to go on with Doctor Johnston. That is the reason I wish to get free from this business; but it is not that I expect Mr. Hamilton to marry me; I know he won't."

The nurse laughed, she thought all this mere affectation on Alice's part, and at all events was glad to have her flirtation with Doctor Johnston brought to a close. " Well, miss," she said, " you are right not to go on writing letters and taking walks with the doctor, at all events. I must be going, Miss Alice."

" Very well, nurse ; you have taken a great deal of trouble, indeed you have."

" No trouble at all, miss," said the old woman, leaving the room.

CHAPTER XIX.

BUT it is not at all times as easy to follow good advice as the givers of it suppose; the old nurse could not see why Alice should give the Johnston love affair another thought, now the doctor was got rid of for the present. But Alice gave it many thoughts; she was not an unfeeling or unprincipled girl by any means; she therefore felt very sorry for the result of her folly, for it now struck her Doctor Johnston might have some grounds for complaining of her conduct. She had listened to his sympathy for her sad position, her loneliness, her stepmother's unkindness; and he had expressed his admiration, his love for her. This seemed nothing at the time—at any moment she fancied she could free herself from such slight bonds as these; but then his letters showed he had begun to expect these meetings as almost a right; and now she had sent messages to him by her father's servant, he had written to her, and he wanted her to meet him again soon, "fearing she might forget." "I did certainly encourage him, I was glad to meet him, I thought of running away with him; I do not see how I shall ever get out of it all," she thought; "and he really does like me, poor fellow;" then Edmund's remembrance intervened, and she dismissed the subject as doubly disagreeable and embarrassing.

Harriet was still very good humoured and gay, she ordered Alice two or three very pretty dresses from her own milliner, she praised her singing, and did all she could to encourage and bring her forward; if this state of things lasted, Alice felt she would have but little to complain of. They arrived at The Grange, without Alice having had any previous interview with Doctor Johnston; but while they were away, the nurse was to see him, and tell him of Alice's imaginary miseries.

Mrs. Hamilton received them very kindly, and Alice could not but like that gentle, soft woman, for to her she appeared in no other light.

Edmund of course was glad to meet her, and they again fell into their old familiar style of conversation, and Edmund loved as before to listen to her singing for him in the evenings. There was a large croquet party expected at Sefton, and they were all asked. Harriet had told Alice that Miss Lowell was a great beauty, and heiress, but as yet she had no idea she was her rival. She looked forward to the party with pleasure, and thought how nicely her new dress would suit for such a gay scene, for the evening was to wind up with a dance, and dances were great novelties to Alice.

The morning of the croquet party was very fine, and Alice was in great spirits, she ran into the garden to gather a bouquet, and thought her appearance complete when she had arranged one. Edmund said, coming in, " Have you not some of the heaths?"

" Oh, no," she said, " is it the heaths!" as if it were a sacrilege ; Edmund walked into the conservatory, and cut her a large bouquet.

" Take these," he said, " and choose the best, it's all folly sparing them. My mother does not care for them, she will be delighted you should take them."

Alice, greatly pleased, discarded her own bouquet.

When they reached Sefton it was crowded, and Alice was delighted with the beauty of the place; there were tents, and the grass was very prettily decorated round the croquet ground; Alice was a very good player, and could appreciate the perfection of the lawn and the implements.

Mrs. Alton met them all at the hall door, and Alice had been wondering which was the heiress, or whether she was present, as they walked to the croquet ground, when a lady in a white dress and jacket, trimmed with blue velvet, who had apparently been playing— for she had a mallet in her hand—walked up to them; how beautiful she is, how graceful, Alice thought, when Harriet said, "Miss Travers, Miss Lowell."

"Oh, I have seen Miss Travers at your ball,

last winter. Do you not remember me? how do you do, I hope you play well. I am getting up another set, I do play so badly myself."

Alice said she played tolerably, of course; and she was introduced to a young officer, who was said to be a most wretched player, that she might take care of him, I presume, She glanced round for Edmund, but he was talking to Ada with such animation, that she was quite too much occupied watching them to pay much further attention to her partner.

" Shew Miss Travers the order we play in, Charlie; don't we begin now?" said Miss Lowell to Alice's companion, who it appeared was Charlie Domville. Edmund of course was Ada's partner.

" What a beautiful girl Miss Lowell is, Mr. Domville," said Alice; " I had no idea she was so handsome—what lovely eyes she has, so expressive, such hazel."

"She is very pretty, she is a cousin of mine. I think her very pretty too."

Then Charlie recollected this would not be a very amusing subject to discuss with Miss Travers, and he began speaking of the beauty of the Spanish women, and of the inhabitants of the different places he had been to during his voyages—as Ada's white dress with its blue markings floated by now and then, Alice would become a little absent; but on the whole they got on very agreeably.

Harriet was looking on, seated on one of the numerous seats around, she did not seem pleased at the attention her brother was paying Ada, and still less at the bright smile with which she listened.

"Come now," she heard her say, "do attend, and get me through some of these hoops, I wish to have an opportunity of looking after our guests, and until my game is finished I cannot." She heard Edmund protesting he would not assist her through a single hoop, would do nothing to hurry the game; and she heard Ada's laughing rejoinders, and saw her sitting down beside her ball on the nearest seat, as if to keep guard over it; but evidently quite ready to excuse Edmund's extraordinary roquets, which generally succeeded in placing them in a worse position than their opponents had left them in; while Ada still sat on the low seat, and chatted to Edmund who was standing beside her.

"I hope that Charlie is amusing Miss Travers," said Ada, "he is such a bad player, if she is fond of the game I am afraid she will be provoked with him. Did you play much at Colonel Travers'?"

"Not once, but no one expects a good game of croquet at a croquet party; you never can get people to play well, the game is so long.

I like a game of six and no lookers on, do you?"

"Yes, I don't wonder you dislike lookers on, if you always roquet as well as you are doing to day, why it is preposterous; there, you have missed my ball again."

"Yes, just so; I was very near striking it. I am sure you and I could play very well, though we, at present I can see, enjoy the reputation of being the greatest of boobies."

"I don't play well, for I seldom played until Charlie came."

"Next day we can have a game then, while he is here, if we can find a partner for him,—Miss Travers perhaps, and I am sure we shall beat them, though I can see Miss Travers plays very well."

"Now do try and hit the ball this time, and let me go. I want to attend to my friends, and you see every one is waiting for us."

Edmund gave the balls a few strokes, and the magic hoop at which they had stopped so long was past; but it was now too late. make what exertions they might, the game was lost; and in a few moments they heard Domville congratulating Miss Travers on its being entirely through her play they had won. Edmund laughed and looked at Ada.

Colonel Travers was walking about with Mrs. Hamilton and Harriet; they had just returned when the game was concluded.

" Oh! papa, think of my having won the game, against such good players, too! Will you just come and look on, and I will show you it all?"

Mrs. Alton met them.

" Alice has been very fortunate, I hear; but you don't care for croquet, I believe, Colonel Travers?"

"I don't understand it, Mrs. Alton; there was no such game in my time."

"Mamma," said Harriet, "would you come here a moment?"

Mrs. Hamilton fell back, and walked beside her daughter.

"Mamma," Harriet said, eagerly, "what do you think? Is Edmund going to be married to Ada? What does he mean by the way he is going on!" she said angrily.

"I suppose so, Harriet; she seems to like him, I think," said the mother, with that affectation of misunderstanding her which made Harriet doubly harsh and rough.

"And what does he mean by flirting with Alice, then? Why, I was sure he would marry her."

"I see no prospect of it to-day. What gave you that idea?"

"Why, he has done nothing but flirt with

the girl," Harriet said, with a great show of indignation. "Does he think I shall bear with such conduct if he will not marry her."

"Everyone flirts ; you should know enough of society, my dear, to admit that; but I see Mrs. Blackall and Kate, I must go and speak to them."

Harriet was full of anger and disappointment ; she now saw that her little contrivance for Alice and Edmund's benefit was not likely to be successful, and she felt too much annoyed not to betray herself to her mother. She was now employed devising what she could do, or considering would she do anything, to overthrow the existing state of things —for she was so much annoyed with Edmund for thwarting her wishes, she would have attempted anything to injure him.

Mrs. Alton met her, and insisted on her joining the next game of croquet ; this, too,

annoyed her—for she would have much preferred watching what everyone was doing, and
thinking over some plan of operation, as
she feared that unless she could at once inter-
pose in some way, her interference would be
to little purpose. She, however, after many
excuses, did join in the game, much against
her will ; but Colonel Travers had seconded
Mrs. Alton's wishes so strongly, that Harriet,
who did not think it politic in anything to
oppose him, assented.

Ada and Edmund were now sitting looking
on ; they applauded the good hits, they laughed
at the mistakes, yet it was all mechanically. I
doubt whether they would have recognised
either, but for the applause or laughter around.

They were really conscious of but one thing
—the presence of each other. Ada was so
grateful for Edmund's friendship, so happy
that he had not met her with coldness, and

estrangement, **that** there **was** a greater softness **and** warmth apparent in her manner than
ever before. In her anxiety to show him how
desirous she **was that they** should remain
friends, she lost the timid fear, which had
previously restrained her from showing her
affection **and** regard for **him.** This friendship—for so she called it—made life really
enjoyable **to her.** She compared him with
others, and the comparison was immensely in
his favour. As they talked together, she **be-**
came more and more conscious of a similarity
of **tastes** and feelings—for Ada was fastidious
in her tastes, as well as romantic in her **feel-**
ings; and she congratulated herself on having
secured the friendship of **one** who could so
completely understand her.

Love, we must remember, **she** had very
sagely concluded she **never had,** would, or
should experience. **Love, it** certainly was

not, which she felt for Edmund; she *merely* wished to monopolize his friendship, to share all his hopes and feelings, that he should rely on her judgment, and be influenced by her wishes.

"I saw Major Bethill's marriage in the papers this morning," said Edmund.

"Yes, so aunt told me; I did not look at the papers to-day."

"The Major would not believe you could take such little interest in his fate. I disliked him so much at one time."

"You had no reason; he seemed very obliging, and people generally liked him. You should not be whimsical."

"I thought I had every reason to dislike him at the time—the evening of our ball; do you remember that evening?"

Edmund had of late adopted a system of

retrospective flirtation—if I may so speak—
he was not to tell Ada how he admired her.
There could be no objection, owing to their
new friendship, in his alluding to how much
he had, at one time, done so, and the jealou-
sies, and sorrows, peculiar to that period; but
which, of course, were in no way connected
with the existing state of things.

"Oh! I remember the ball. Do you play
as much as you did then? You lost a great
deal at cards one evening."

"I never play; I had never in my life
played for more than a few shillings, or some
mere trifle, I mean, before that night at the
Barracks. Who told you I lost so much?"
he said.

"One hears all those things; but you should
not—that poor boy, he cannot escape being
ruined."

" Major Bethill encouraged it too much, certainly; in the commanding officer it's a very bad example, and the young fellows are almost sure to take it up. Gaynor is a fool, I think."

" Did he play much?" said Ada; " I mean Major Bethill ?"

" Oh! every night, a rubber of whist, and anything else going; he liked *ecarté* very well, and loo—Cole is fond of it, too. Now, was it not the Major who told you I lost that evening ? I am sure it was."

" You think people chat a great deal while they are dancing ?"

" Oh ! he was talking to you in the conservatory, do you not remember ? And now I am sure he was telling you of all our doings at the Barracks. I wondered what that long conversation was about at the time. I had fancied it was something very romantic, I assure you."

" Oh! had you; there is no romance about the Major."

" You should not say so of one of your own victims."

" Miss Travers is a very nice girl, I think; is she clever? I think there is something engaging in her manner. What a good roquet that last of hers."

" Yes, she is ; I liked her very much; we rode together almost every day while I was at Horton. She sings well."

" I must ask her to sing this evening. And you rode a good deal together?"

" We never had the meet here. Fortune was kind, you see. You were very decided about that riding, Miss Lowell. I must try never to forget how you refused me."

Ada laughed.

" We must be very good friends, and you must not forget," she said.

" I have such a bad memory, I am sure I shall forget. You must remind me occasionally. If I asked you to dance this evening, should you be angry and think I had forgotten ?"

" I should not be angry; I should not think you had forgotten."

" Why did you spoil the sentence ? The first part has been anything but improved by your adding to it. Charlie Domville is to have the first dance, is he not ?"

" How do you know ? But—yes, he is— at least, he asked me yesterday."

" Oh ! he tells me a great many things; he told me that—but the second ; the second has not been promised."

"The second has not. And Charlie told you that? He is a queer fellow, is he not? but such a good fellow."

"He is; I like him greatly. He told me he was trying to get the Victoria Cross—at least, I mean that he had applied. He must be a dashing fellow to have a claim for it ; and do you know it's all that you may know he deserved it."

Ada blushed.

"I should be so glad," she said, "he would be quite a hero. What did he do? What is he to get it for?"

"I will let him tell you that himself, it would be very unfair not—that was a very bad shot — but you have not promised me the second ; is it gone also?"

" Oh ! yes, you shall have the second. You know Miss Blackall will be here, so you will have plenty of dancing, I am sure."

"She can be jealous," thought Edmund, "even of a friend; this friendship is delightful."

END OF VOL. I.

T. C. NEWBY, 30, Welbeck Street, Cavendish Square, London.